The Pre

I was shrinking as I morphed, falling, falling, falling down into the water which had been around my thighs and was now around my neck.

I had the terrifying sensation of knowing that all the bones inside my body were dissolving, as a hard, fingernail-like crust covered me all over.

My human body was melting away.

My human vision was fading. I could no longer see the way a human sees.

Which was a good thing, because I really did not want to see what I was becoming . . .

Even the book morphs!
Flip the pages
and check it out!

Look for other ANIMORPHS titles
by K.A. Applegate:

1 The Invasion
2 The Visitor
3 The Encounter
4 The Message

And coming soon:

6 The Capture

ANIMORPHS

The Predator

K.A. Applegate

Hippo

For Michael

Quote from p59 of JOURNEY TO THE ANTS by Bert Holldobler and Edward O. Wilson. Copyright © 1994 by Bert Holldobler and Edward O. Wilson. Reprinted by permission of Harvard University Press.

Scholastic Children's Books,
Commonwealth House, 1 – 19 New Oxford Street, London WC1A 1NU, UK
a division of Scholastic Ltd
London ~ New York ~ Toronto ~ Sydney ~ Auckland

First published in the USA by Scholastic Inc., 1996
First published in the UK by Scholastic Ltd, 1997

ISBN 0 590 19323 6

Printed by Cox & Wyman Ltd, Reading, Berks.

10 9 8 7 6 5 4 3 2 1

Chapter 1

My name is Marco.

I can't tell you my last name or where I live. Believe me, I wish I could. I would like nothing more than to be able to tell you my name is Marco Jones or Williams or Vasquez or Brown or Anderson or McCain.

Marco McCain. Has kind of a nice sound, doesn't it?

But McCain's not my last name. I'm not even going to swear to you that *Marco* is my first name. See, I'm hoping to live for a while longer. I'm not going to make it any easier for the Yeerks to find me.

I live in a paranoid world. But just because I'm paranoid doesn't mean I don't have enemies.

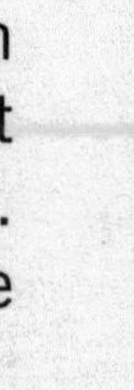

I have *real* enemies. Enemies that would freeze your blood if you only knew.

So, see, I'd really like to tell you my name, and address, and phone number, too, because if I could do that, it would mean I no longer had any enemies. It would mean my life was normal again. It would mean I could go back to minding my own business.

I believe in minding my own business.

Which is why what happened on my way home from the 7-Eleven was so dumb.

I was walking down the street with some low-fat milk, a loaf of bread and a bag of peanut M&M's. Since my mum died, I've been stuck with a lot of the shopping and stuff for my dad and me.

This 7-Eleven isn't exactly in the greatest neighbourhood, so I was walking kind of fast, minding my own business, trying not to think about the fact that it was after ten at night.

Then I heard it.

"Just don't hurt me, just don't hurt me."

It was a man's voice. An old man, from the sound of it. It was coming from a dark alley.

I hesitated. I stopped. I pressed myself back against the cold brick wall of the building and listened.

"Just gimme the money, old man, don't make me hurt you," a second voice said. A younger voice. A tough voice.

"I gave you all of it!" the old man cried.

Then the thug said something I can't repeat. Basically, he was getting ready to pound the old man. I heard other voices. Three thugs total. It didn't look good for the old man.

"This is totally *not* your problem, Marco," I told myself. "Stay out of it. Don't be an idiot."

Three thugs. Each of them probably twice as big as I was. I'm not exactly Arnold Schwarzenegger. I'm not even average height for my age, although I make up for it by being incredibly cute.

And charming. And witty. And modest.

But I was pretty sure the three gang members in that alley were not going to be very impressed by my cuteness.

Fortunately, I have other abilities.

It had been some while since I had done this particular morph, but as I concentrated, I could feel it coming back. I slipped into the opening of the alley and hid in the shadow of a very smelly, very large dustbin.

The first thing that happened was the fur. It sprouted quickly from my arms and legs and all down my body. Thick, rough, ragged, black fur. It grew long on my arms and back and head. It was shorter everywhere else.

My jaw bulged forward. I could hear the bones in my jaw grind as they stretched and the non-

human DNA changed my body.

Morphing doesn't hurt. It creeps you out sometimes, but it doesn't hurt. And as morphs go, this one wasn't bad. I mean, I still got to keep all my usual arms and legs and stuff. Not like when I morphed into an osprey. Or a dolphin. I mean, when I was a dolphin, I was breathing through a hole in the back of my neck.

With this morph I had arms, as usual. Only they were a lot bigger. A *lot* bigger. My legs bent forward. My shoulders grew so massive it was like having a couple of pigs sitting on my back. I also had an enormous round belly and a leathery chest.

My face was a black, bulging, rubbery mask, and my eyes were practically invisible beneath my heavy brow.

I had become a gorilla.

Now, here's the thing about gorillas. They are the sweetest animals around. If you leave them alone they will mostly just sit and eat leaves all day.

And that's all the gorilla mind really wanted to do right then — eat some leaves, maybe a nice piece of fruit.

But I was inside that head, too, along with the gorilla's instincts. And I had decided to teach those thugs a little lesson. See, now that I was in that gorilla body, I weighed two hundred kilos.

And I was mighty strong.

How strong? Let me put it this way. Compared to a gorilla, a human being is made out of toothpicks. I wasn't just twice as strong as a man, I was maybe four, five, six times stronger.

Further down the alley, the three thugs had lost patience with the old man.

"Just give him a kicking," one of the geniuses said.

That's when I decided to say hello. To get their attention, I picked up the dustbin and threw it against the far wall of the alley.

Yes, that enormous dustbin.

CRASH! BOOM!

"What was that?"

"Look! What *is* that thing?"

"Whoa! That's some kind of a . . . of a monkey!"

Monkey! I thought. *Excuse me? Monkey? I'll show you monkey.*

Before they could decide what to do, I charged. Knuckles scraping the dirty ground, small hind legs propelling me forward, I charged.

If the thugs had had any sense, they would have run.

They didn't.

"Get it!" one yelled.

I grabbed his arm with one massive fist. I

lifted him straight off the ground and threw him over my shoulder.

"Aaaaaaahhhhh!"

BOOMPH!

He landed on the ground behind me. The other two rushed at me, one on the left, one on the right. I saw a knife glittering. The knife slashed my arm. It almost hurt.

"Hoo hooo hrrraaawwwrr!" I yelled, in pure gorilla.

With my injured arm, I landed a backhand blow to the knife guy's chest. He flew back. I mean, *flew.* He hit the wall and dropped.

I just grabbed the third guy by the shirt collar and threw him into the dustbin.

"Don't kill meeeee!" he cried as he sailed through the air.

I had no intention of killing anyone. I hoisted the knife guy into the dustbin with his friend. He wasn't breathing real well, but I figured he'd survive.

Hah, I thought. *Who needs Spiderman, when Marco is on the case?*

While I was telling myself just how cool I was, I heard the sound.

It was a click. Two clicks, actually. The sound of an automatic pistol being cocked.

I spun around.

BLAM! BLAM!

It was the first guy. The one I'd thrown over my shoulder. He was up on his feet, gun pointed.

I was big. I was powerful. But a gun was a whole different story. And loud! Man, are those things loud.

"Hah! Come and get some, monkey man!"

I barrelled behind the dustbin. I leaned my massive shoulders into it and sent it rolling and spinning and sliding at the guy with the gun.

"Ahhhhh!"

BLAMPH!

So much for the guy with the gun.

I checked. He was alive. He wasn't happy, but he was alive. The gun was nowhere to be seen.

Well, Marco, I thought, *that went OK. Now, find somewhere private, demorph, call 911 to come arrest these guys, and you can still get home in time to watch* Letterman.

Unfortunately, I had forgotten one thing.

"G-g-get out of here you . . . you *monster*!"

The old man. The one I had risked my life to save. He stood, facing me. He was shaking with fear and red in the face.

Oh, I thought. *So* that's *where the gun went.*

The old man was pointing the gun at me.

"Back, you demon! Don't come any closer."

BLAM! BLAM! BLAM!

I tore out of the alley with bullets whizzing through the air.

Which just goes to show why you should never get involved in other people's problems.

Chapter 2

"Yeah, so then I do the gorilla thing, right? I save the old man. I'm the hero. I *am* Spiderman. I *am* Wolverine. I *am* Batman —"

"Or at least Gorilla Boy," Rachel interrupted.

She did a forward flip as we walked across the springy grass. Rachel's into gymnastics. It's very distracting when someone forward flips while they're talking to you.

It was the day after my big hero act. We were all out in a far meadow of Cassie's farm — me, Jake, Cassie, and Rachel, strolling through little bunches of wildflowers. Tobias was flying overhead, about thirty metres up, in a sky dotted with bright, white clouds.

"And what happens as I am playing Captain

America?" I ask. "The old man unloads the gun at me. I totally lost the milk and my bag of M&M's."

Jake gave me a disgruntled look. "Marco? It was good of you to rescue the old man. But you really shouldn't be turning into a gorilla."

Now, as you're reading this, you're probably thinking, *Um, Marco? Time out. You've left out a few things. Like, how can you turn into a gorilla?*

Good question.

It happened on a dark night when we were all heading home from the shopping mall. There were five of us.

Me, you already know.

Jake is my best friend, even though, unfortunately, he is kind of a pain sometimes. He's one of those serious-type guys. You just say the word "responsibility" and he snaps to attention. He's the kind of guy who always seems like he's bigger than he actually is. That's because he has that whole "I'm in charge, and you can trust me" thing going on. He has sensible brown hair, and trustworthy brown eyes, and one of those strong confident chins.

He also has a great sense of humour and is very smart, and I would trust him with my life any day, any time. Not that I would ever tell *him* that.

Then there's Cassie. I didn't really know her very well back then. But I think she's kind of

Jake's girlfriend now. Of course, none of us is supposed to know this. *Ssshhh!* Big secret!

Cassie is the one who is least like me. If I'm comedy, she's poetry. She's a natural peace-maker. She's the one who knows when you're feeling bad and will find something nice to say that makes you feel better. And it's not like she's manipulating. She really cares about things. She's like sincere or something.

Cassie is our animal expert. Her parents are both vets and she spends most of her free time helping her dad run the Wildlife Rehabilitation Clinic. It's in the barn at their farm. They rescue injured woodchucks and deer and eagles and so on. Cassie actually knows how to get an injured, angry wolf to take its pills. (Not an easy thing. Believe me. I *was* a wolf once.)

If you go out to her barn you'll see this little, short, black girl in overalls and boots with her arm halfway down the throat of a wolf that could just bite it right off. And she'll be smiling and acting like it's no big deal. And the wolf will be just standing there, looking like he's trying to earn a gold star for being the best little boy in school.

Then there's Rachel. Very beautiful. Very leggy-blonde-supermodel type. Ms Fashion. Ms Properly-Applied-Makeup. Ms Has-It-All — Looks-*and*-Brains.

Rachel is Jake's cousin, and a total babe who, unfortunately, is also totally insane. See, somehow, underneath all that perfect hair and perfect teeth, there's this lunatic Amazon warrior-queen, just fighting to get out.

Here's what Rachel'll say whenever we decide to do something so dangerous it makes you want to wet yourself: "I'm in! Let's go! Let's do it!"

I swear that, if she could, Rachel would be wearing a suit of armour and swinging a sword. And it would be a fashionable suit of armour, and she would look great in it.

Then there is Tobias. That night in the construction site, he was just this kind of dweeby kid I barely knew. He liked Jake because Jake once kept some guys from beating him up.

To be honest with you, I don't even remember what Tobias looked like back then. Now, of course, he looks like a fierce, angry bird of prey.

There's a downside to the morphing power we have. A time limit of two hours. Stay more than two hours in a morph, and you stay forever.

That's why Tobias was flying overhead, with his wide wings spread, catching the warm updrafts. Tobias is a hawk. A red-tail hawk, to be exact. I guess he always will be.

I tease Tobias sometimes.

What happened to him scares me.

Anyway, on that night we were cutting through

this big, abandoned construction site. It was supposed to be a shopping centre, but they got it half built and then stopped.

Then, to cut a long story short, there was this spaceship. It was carrying an Andalite who was dying of wounds he'd got fighting the Yeerks up in Earth orbit. Or thereabouts.

He's the one who told us about the Yeerks. The Yeerks are parasites. They use the bodies of other species. They take them over. They control them. That's what you call a human who's been taken over — a Controller. A human Controller.

Jake's brother, Tom, is one. A Controller.

And Melissa, Rachel's friend, her father is one, too.

The Andalites fight the Yeerks. They had been trying to stop the secret Yeerk invasion of Earth, but basically they got wiped out. Before he died, the Andalite promised us that reinforcements would come. Eventually. In the meantime, all he could do for us was give us a weapon.

That weapon was the power to morph. To acquire the DNA of any animal we could touch, and then to *become* that animal.

So that was the deal. Just the five of us, five regular everyday kids, were supposed to fight the Yeerks alone until the Andalites came along and rescued us.

Five kids versus the Yeerks. The Yeerks, who

had already conquered the terrifying Hork-Bajir and made them into Controllers. The Yeerks, with their creepy allies, the Taxxon-Controllers. The Yeerks, who were now infiltrating human society, making Controllers out of cops and teachers and soldiers and mayors and TV newspeople. They were everywhere. They could be anyone.

And all we had was five kids who could turn into birds.

Or gorillas.

"I just don't think we should be morphing out on the street in order to get involved in stopping everyday crimes," Jake lectured me. "Remember what happened at the used car lot with Rachel and Tobias — and you asked them if they were insane!"

I was about to argue when Rachel spoke up again.

"I think Marco did the right thing," she said. "What was he supposed to do? Just walk away? I don't think so."

"OK, now I *know* I was wrong," I said. "Any time Rachel thinks I did the right thing, it has to be wrong. Besides, that was my whole point. I risked my life for that old man, and I don't even get a thank you."

"I don't know if it was a good idea," Cassie said, "but the feeling behind it was good. I think it was heroic."

Well, what could I say to that? It's very hard to disagree with someone who has just called you a hero.

Jake decided to let it go. Unfortunately, the reason he decided to drop it was that he had something bigger to talk about.

He got his serious look.

I groaned. I hate that serious look. It always means trouble.

"Jake? Are you going to tell me why we're all out walking in the fields together? Aside from the fact that it's a nice day and all?"

"We're going to see Ax," Jake explained. "Cassie and I have been talking to him the last couple of days. You know, about what he wants to do."

"Uh-oh," I muttered quietly. "I just know I'm not going to like this."

"Well . . . probably not. Ax wants to go home," Jake said.

"Home?" Rachel repeated.

"To the Andalite home world," Cassie said.

Ax, whose real name is Aximili-Esgarrouth-Isthil, is an Andalite.

I stopped walking. The others stopped, too. "Um, excuse me, but isn't the Andalite home world kind of far away?"

"Ax says it's about eighty-two light years," Jake confirmed.

"Light travels about three hundred thousand kilometres per *second*," I pointed out. "Times sixty seconds per minute. Times sixty minutes per hour. Times twenty-four hours per day. Times three hundred and sixty-five days per year. That's one light year. Times eighty-two years."

Rachel laughed. "So you *have* been staying awake in science class, Marco."

"We tried to figure it out in kilometres. But none of our calculators go that high," Jake said.

"You know, Jake, I could be wrong, but I don't think any of the major airlines fly to the Andalite home world," I said.

"Uh-huh," he said with a nod. "I know. That's why we'll have to steal a Yeerk spaceship."

Chapter 3

"There he is," Cassie said.

I followed the direction of her gaze. Way over towards the line of trees at the edge of the field, I saw him.

Ax.

The Andalite.

From a distance you'd think he was a small horse or a deer. He has four hooved feet that flash with amazing speed. His upper body looks like a horse's neck and head, except that when he gets close enough, you see that he has two smaller, human-sized arms sticking out.

His head is kind of a triangle, with two huge, almond-shaped eyes. Those are his main eyes. There are two extra eyes, each stuck atop a sort

of stalk. The stalks stick out of the top of his head and move around, pointing the extra eyes in any direction.

But the thing that really makes you stare is the tail.

According to Cassie and Rachel, Ax is cute. I wouldn't know, being a guy. All I know is, when you see that curved tail, you know right away that Andalites aren't exactly cuddly koalas or little puppies.

The Andalite tail resembles a scorpion's tail. It curls up and over, and is armed with a wicked scythe blade. They can strike with those tails faster than your eye can see.

I'd seen the first Andalite do it. In the last seconds before the evil creature known as Visser Three murdered the Andalite prince, he had struck with that tail again and again.

That memory came back to me as I watched Ax galloping towards us, tail arched and ready.

"I hope there's no one around," Jake said anxiously. He scanned the area. It was pretty remote. Cassie's house and barn were way out of sight. And there was no reason why anyone would be in this distant field.

I looked up and saw Tobias's reddish tail feathers. I gave him a wave.

<All clear,> Tobias called down to us in thought-speak. <There's some people having a

picnic, but that's a couple of kilometres from here.>

Ax came galloping up. <Prince Jake!> he said, also in thought-speak.

Jake groaned. Ax had got it into his head that Jake was our leader, which was partly true. And I guess for an Andalite, any leader is some kind of prince.

Ax has no mouth. No one had asked him yet how he ate with no mouth.

He communicates by thought-speech. It's the same way we communicate when we're morphed. For us humans it *only* works when we're morphed. For Andalites, it's the normal way to communicate.

"Hi, Ax," Jake said, as the Andalite came to a skidding stop just a few metres from us. "How are you doing?"

<I am well. And each of you?>

"I'm fine," Cassie said.

Tobias swooped down out of the sky. He braked and landed neatly on the grass.

"I'm fine, too, Ax," I said. "Or at least I was until I thought I heard someone say something really stupid."

Ax looked uncertain. He swivelled one of his stalk eyes forward to get a better look at me. <What stupid thing was said?>

"Someone said we were going to try and steal

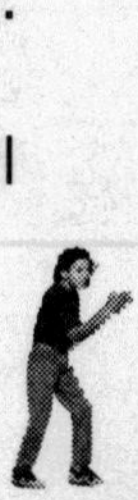

a Yeerk spaceship," I said.

He smiled an Andalite smile, which is hard to describe, except that it involves his main eyes. <You think it will be dangerous?>

"Dangerous? No, jumping off a ten-storey building is dangerous. Sticking your tongue in an electrical socket is dangerous — not to mention painful. But stealing a Yeerk ship is beyond dangerous."

<The higher the danger, the higher the honour,> Ax said. <Is this not true?>

I gave Rachel a sidelong look. "I think we've found your future husband."

"It may be honourable to try and get a Yeerk ship, Ax," Jake said, "but honour *isn't* our most important goal."

The Andalite looked surprised — I think. His main eyes widened, and his stalk eyes stretched up to their maximum height. It looked a bit like surprise to me.

<What else do you fight for, if not honour?>

Jake shrugged. "Look, we're trying to do what we can to hurt the Yeerks. But we're also trying to stay alive. We're all there is. I mean, no one else even knows there is a Yeerk invasion. So if something happens to us . . ." He let it hang.

<I did not mean to offend,> Ax said. <You are right, of course. You are alone. If you fail, all is lost.>

"So the question is whether this is something we can do without getting killed," Jake pointed out.

"Yeah, we're mostly against getting killed," I added. "So how are we supposed to grab a Yeerk ship? They're up in orbit. We're down here. It's not like we can call them up and ask them to come down."

<Yes, we can do that,> Ax said.

"What?"

<We can call them.>

"Right."

<I can create a Yeerk distress beacon. They will send a ship to investigate.>

"You mean like, 'Hello? Hello? Is this Visser Three? Could you send a ship down to pick me up?'" I said.

I expected everyone to laugh because the idea was so totally ridiculous. No one laughed.

"Um, excuse me?" I said, trying again. "Personally, I have had plenty of Visser Three in my life. I don't need to call him on the phone."

<It will not involve that . . . that foul beast,> Ax said.

That was one thing I liked about Ax. He hated Visser Three. He reminded me of the Andalite prince, who was Ax's older brother. When either of them said the word "Yeerk," let alone "Visser Three," you could just feel the air

vibrating from their anger.

<It will be a minor matter,> Ax said. <They will hear a distress beacon and send a Bug fighter to investigate.>

"There is always at least one Hork-Bajir and one Taxxon aboard each Bug fighter," I pointed out. "Any time you start playing with Hork-Bajirs, it's not a minor thing."

<Do you fear them?> Ax demanded. He stared at me with all four eyes.

"You better believe I fear them."

<Fear is unworthy of a warrior.>

He seemed a little too determined for me. I don't know much about Andalites, but I had a feeling I understood this one, at least a little. See, he was alive. But every other Andalite who had come to Earth, including Ax's brother, the prince, was dead.

So I took a shot. It wasn't fair, maybe, but he'd made me mad, acting like I was some kind of coward. "How many times have you fought Hork-Bajir? Or any other Controller?" I asked him.

His stalk eyes drooped. He pawed the ground with one hoof. <Never,> he said.

I nodded. "I thought so. So let me tell you something, Ax. It's scary. It's so scary that sometimes you wish you could just go ahead and die because it's easier than dealing with the terror."

Well, I thought as I looked around at my friends, *that pretty well killed everyone's happy mood.*

It was Tobias who broke the silence. <If you get a Yeerk ship, can you get back to the Andalite home world?>

Ax seemed abashed, but he answered, <Yes. I hope so.>

<And if you make it, can you do anything to hurry your people up? To get them back here quicker?>

<I am young. Like you. But I am the brother of Prince Elfangor. My people will listen to me. I . . . I know that they will come, either way. But yes, perhaps if I can return and tell them how desperate your situation is . . .>

Jake took a deep breath. "OK. Time for a vote."

I groaned. I already knew what it would be.

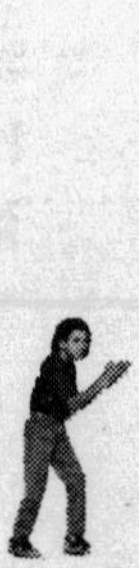

Chapter 4

"OK, ready?" I asked.

<Yes. I am prepared to begin the morph,> Ax said.

It was Saturday. A couple of days after we had all agreed to go ahead with the plan to capture a Yeerk ship. We were in Cassie's barn, surrounded by cages full of injured animals and birds. Cassie's father and mother were both away for the day.

Jake checked his watch. "Ten past ten," he reported.

"Ax starts morphing at ten-twelve and is done by ten-fifteen. The bus will be at the stop at ten twenty-five," I said. "It will arrive at the mall at eleven. By that point Ax will have been in morph for forty-five minutes. That leaves an hour and fifteen minutes on the two-hour morph time."

"Is it enough time?" Cassie wondered. She was biting her lip nervously.

I shrugged. "Thirty minutes to reach Radio Shack, find the bits that Ax needs to make his transmitter, buy them and get back to catch the eleven-thirty bus home. That gets back here at five past twelve. Ten minutes to spare."

Jake was looking pretty stony-faced, which is how he looks when he's not sure if something will work.

"It's the best we can do," I said.

"I know. Everyone ready?" Jake asked.

"I should go *with* you guys," Rachel said for like the tenth time that morning. "I should be there."

"No. We can't *all* go. If something goes wrong, we don't want everyone caught at once," I said. "And something is sure to go wrong."

<Why do you say that?!> Ax demanded sharply.

Jake smiled at him. "Marco doesn't believe in optimism."

Tobias flew almost silently into the barn through the open hayloft. <It's still all clear. And the bus is right on schedule, just coming down Margolis Avenue.>

"OK, Ax. Time to morph," Jake said.

"And, um, don't forget the morphing outfit, OK?" I reminded him. The concept of clothing kind of puzzled the Andalite. We'd got him skintight bike shorts and a T-shirt that he could use for morphing, but he still didn't know why.

It's one of the most annoying things about morphing — dealing with clothing. We'd learned how to morph clothing, but only things that were really tight-fitting. Any time you tried to morph a jacket or sweater they just ended up shredded. And shoes? Forget about shoes.

<Clothing, yes,> he said. <I have integrated it into my human morph.>

"Time," Jake said, pointing at his watch.

Ax began to change.

I'd only seen him do it once before — soon after we rescued him from the sunken Andalite dome ship.

Now I've seen a lot of morphing. I've done a lot of it, too. It's always creepy watching a human being become some strange animal. But watching Ax morph was different. He wasn't becoming an animal. He was becoming a human being.

The stalk eyes shrank and disappeared in his head. The deadly scorpion tail shrivelled and withered and slithered up inside him like someone sucking up a piece of spaghetti.

His front hooves disappeared completely.

"Whoa, look out," Jake said. He caught the

Andalite as he fell forward, with no front legs to support him.

<Thank you. I must practise standing with only two legs.>

A gash opened in his face and grew lips and teeth. A nose grew where there had just been small vertical slits. His eyes became smaller, more human.

But the weirdest thing about Ax morphing was not just that he looked like a human. It was that he looked like a *particular* human.

Actually, *four* particular humans. See, he had absorbed DNA from Jake and Cassie and Rachel and me. Somehow, by some process we did not understand, he was able to combine our genetic patterns to come up with one person.

The end result was definitely strange and disturbing.

I looked at him and saw some of myself, and Jake, and Rachel and Cassie, too, although Ax was male. That was the most bizarre part. Looking at him and thinking, *Hey, he looks familiar. Really familiar. In fact, hey, that's* my *hair!*

"Ax, you could be either a really pretty guy, or a kind of unattractive girl," I said.

"I am an Andalite," he said. "Andalite. Lite. Ite."

"OK, put on those additional clothes," Jake said. "Let's get going. Tobias?" He looked up to

the rafters.

<On my way. I'll check on the bus,> Tobias said, and flew away.

"More clothing? Clo. Clo-theeeeng. Clo-theeng?" Ax said.

"Ax? Don't do that," I said.

"What? Wha wha wha. Tuh."

"That. Where you play with the sounds. Just say what you need to say, and stop."

Like I said, the Andalites have no mouths and no spoken speech. Ax seemed to think mouths were some kind of toy.

"Yes," Ax agreed. "Yah. Ess."

"And one other thing? The shoes go on your feet. Not in your pockets."

"Yes. I remember. Mem. Ber." He pulled his trainers out of his pockets and looked at them helplessly. Rachel and Cassie each took a foot and got him laced up.

"People are going to think he's weird," Rachel said, sounding exasperated.

"Fortunately, it's the mall on a Saturday morning," I pointed out. "It'll be full of weird people."

"Not *this* weird," Rachel said. "This could be trouble."

"Isn't it a little late for you to admit that I was right and this idea is insane?" I asked her. "Besides, no need to worry. I'll be there."

"Great. Then it's sure to be a disaster."

We caught the bus without any problem. Ax made strange mouth noises the entire trip, but the bus was mostly empty.

We got to the mall right on time.

"So far, so good," Jake said as we headed into the mall.

I rolled my eyes. "Jake? Do me a favour. Don't ever say 'so far, so good.' The only time anyone *ever* says 'so far, so good' is right before everything blows up in his face."

"So far. So far. Farrrrr. Faaaar," Ax said, trying out the sounds. "So. Sssso far so so so good."

"Oh, man," I said.

Chapter 5

The mall was a zoo. Wall-to-wall with people. Old people moving real slow. Married people with squalling babies in big huge buggies. High school kids trying to look cool. Mall security trying to look tough. Good-looking girls carrying bags from The Limited.

Your basic Saturday at the mall.

"OK, where is Radio Shack?" Jake wondered.

"I don't know," I said.

"Is it up on the second level? You know, down by Sears?"

"Is that it? Or is that Circuit City?"

"Let me check the map over there. Ax? Come on with . . ." Jake stopped suddenly. "Marco? Where is Ax?"

I spun around. "He was right here!"

Bodies everywhere! All I saw were bodies. Men, women, boys, girls, babies. But no aliens. At least not that I could see. We had lost Ax!

It had taken a total of about two minutes for us to mess up.

Then, suddenly, I saw a strangely familiar face.

"There he is! On the escalator!"

"How did he get all the way over there?" Jake demanded.

We took off after him, but it was so crowded we could barely move. Jake started pushing his way through. I grabbed him by the arm.

"Don't run, man. The security guards will think you're ripping something off. Besides, we can't attract attention. Controllers shop, too."

Jake slowed instantly. "You're right. This many people, some of them are sure to be Controllers."

We threaded our way, moving as quickly as we could without being too obvious. I just kept saying "excuse me, excuse me," and tried not to bump into anyone who looked like he'd get mad and pound me.

It seemed to take forever to reach the escalator. By then we had totally lost sight of Ax.

"As long as he doesn't demorph we're OK," Jake said. "I mean, what's the worst he could do?"

"Jake, I don't want to think about the worst he could do," I said.

"There!"

"Where?"

"Over at Starbucks. The coffee place."

I'm not as tall as Jake so I couldn't see him as easily. But as we got near Starbucks, I spotted him. He was standing patiently in line.

We got to him just in time to hear him say, "I'll have . . . I-yull, Ile, have a double latte, too. Double. Bull. Bull. Latay ay ay."

"He must have heard someone else say it," I whispered to Jake.

"Caff or decaf?" the clerk asked.

Ax stared. "Caff? Caff caff caff?"

"That will be two ninety-five."

Ax stared some more. "Fi-ive."

Jake reached into his pocket and yanked out the money he'd brought to pay for the things at Radio Shack. "Here you go," he said, peeling off three dollars.

I took Ax's arm gently and guided him to the counter. "Ax, *don't* go off on your own, OK? We almost lost you."

"Lost? I am here. Hee-yar."

"Yeah, look, just stay close, OK?" I gave Jake a look. "See? It's your fault. You said, 'so far, so good.'"

The Starbucks guy handed Ax a paper cup.

Ax took it. He looked around to see what the other people were doing. Like them, he put a lid on his cup.

Then, still mimicking the others, he attempted to drink.

"Um, Ax?" I said. "You have to drink where the little hole is in the lid."

"A hole! In the lid! No spills! Ills!"

This was the coolest thing Ax had ever seen. I guess coffee cup technology hasn't advanced very far on the Andalite home planet. Probably because they don't have mouths, and so drinking is not a big concern. But whatever the reason, Ax wouldn't shut up about it.

"So simple! Imple. And yet so effective!"

"Yeah, it's a miracle of human technology," I said.

"I have wanted to try other mouth uses. Drinking. Eating." Then, as an afterthought, he added, "Eeee-ting. Ting."

"Just line the little hole on the top up with your mouth," I said. "Come on, there's Radio Shack. We've already lost like ten minutes."

The two of us hemmed Ax in and herded him towards Radio Shack.

Then he drank the coffee.

"Ahhh! Ohhh! Oh, oh, oh, what? What? What is that?!"

"What?" I asked, alarmed. I swivelled my

head back and forth, looking for some danger.

"A new sense. It . . . I cannot explain it. It is . . . it comes from this mouth." He pointed at his mouth. "It happened when I drank the liquid. It was pleasant. Very pleasant."

It took a few seconds for Jake and I to realize what he was talking about. "Oh. Taste! He's tasting it," Jake said. "He doesn't normally have the sense of taste."

"At least he stopped repeating sounds," I muttered.

"Taste," Ax said, contradicting me. "Aste. Tuh-aste."

He drank his coffee and we got him to Radio Shack. "OK, look, Ax, we have very little time. See if the stuff you need is here."

I'll say this for Ax. He may have been a little weird by human standards, but the boy knows his technology. I mean, he went down the pegboards in the back of the store and just started lifting off different components.

"This must be a primitive *gairtmof,*" he said, inspecting a small switch. "And this could be a sort of *fleer.* Very primitive, but it will work."

In ten minutes' time he'd accumulated a dozen components, ranging from coaxial cable to batteries to things I didn't even recognize.

"Good," he said at last. "All I lack is a Z-Space transponder. Transponder. PONder."

"A what?"

"A Z-Space transponder. It translates the signal into zero space."

I looked at Jake. "Zero space?"

Jake looked back at me and shrugged. "Never heard of it."

Ax looked doubtful. "Zero space," he repeated. "Zeeeero. The opposite of true space. Anti-reality." He looked patiently from one of us to the other. "Zero space, the nondimension where faster-than-light travel is possible. Bull. Possi-bull-uh."

"Oh," I said sarcastically. "*That* zero space. Um, Ax? Sorry to be so primitive and all, but we don't have faster-than-light travel. And I've never heard of zero space."

"Oh."

"Yeah. *Oh.*"

"Let's get this stuff and worry about the other thing later," Jake said calmly. But I could tell he was getting slightly hacked off. "I'll go pay for this stuff."

Ax drained the last of his coffee. "Taste," he said. "I would like more taste." He cocked his head. "I smell things. I believe . . . buh-leeve . . . bleeve . . . there is a connection between smell and taste."

"Yeah, you're right," I said. "We can't travel faster than light, but we can make a sticky bun

that smells pretty good."

"Sticky," Ax said. "Must I carry this?" he asked, indicating his empty coffee cup.

"No, you can just throw it away."

Bad choice of words. Ax threw the coffee cup. Hard. It hit one of the cashiers in the head.

"Hey!"

"Sorry, it was an accident, man," I yelped, rushing to the cashier. "He's . . . he's sick. He, um, has this condition. You know, like out-of-control spasms."

Jake said, "Yeah, it's not his fault. It's like a seizure!"

The clerk rubbed his head. "OK, forget it. Besides, he's out of here and that's all I care about."

"He's what?"

Jake and I turned fast. But Ax was gone.

Jake grabbed the bag of stuff and raced after me out into the stream of people.

Ax was nowhere to be seen.

But then I looked down at the lower level. There was a crowd of people kind of surging. All moving in the same direction. Like they were running to see something.

"They're heading towards the food court," Jake said.

"Oh, I have a *very* bad feeling about this," I said.

We ran for the escalator. We shoved down it, yelling "excuse me" every two seconds.

We got to the food court. We wormed our way through a crowd of laughing, giggling, pointing people.

And there, all alone — because all the sane people had pulled away — was Ax.

He was racing like some lunatic from table to table, snatching up leftover food and shoving it in his mouth.

As I watched he grabbed a half-eaten slice of pizza.

"Taste!" he yelled as he took a huge bite. He threw the rest of the pizza through the air. It just missed the security guard who was closing in on him.

Ax couldn't care less. He had found a piece of Cinnabun. "This was the smell!" he cried. He jammed the roll in his mouth. "Ahhh! Ahhh! Taste! Taste! Wonderful! Ful. Ful."

"They *do* make a good sticky bun," I muttered to Jake.

"We have to get him out of here," Jake hissed.

"Too late. Look! Three more security guards."

The guards jumped at Ax.

Ax decided it was a good time to throw the rest of the bun away. It hit the nearest guard in the face.

"Ax! Run! Run!" I yelled.

I guess I got through, because Ax ran.

Unfortunately, he couldn't run very well in his two-legged human morph.

So as he ran and stumbled, chased by huffing, puffing security guards, he began to change.

Chapter 6

"Stop!" a guard yelled. "I am ordering you to halt!"

But Ax wasn't interested in halting. He was panicked.

A woman stepped out of the Body Shop holding a bag full of colourful jars. Ax ploughed into her. The bag went flying.

The stalks began to grow out of the top of his head. The extra eyes appeared on the ends and turned backward to watch the people chasing him.

Jake and I were two of those people. We were ahead of security, but not by much. Fortunately, I guess the guards assumed we were just idiots running along for fun.

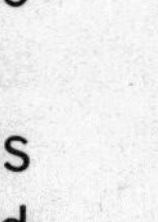

I could hear one of the guards yelling into his walkie-talkie. "Cut him off at the east entrance!"

Legs began to grow out from the chest of Ax's human morph. His own front legs, small at first, but growing rapidly.

He was slowing down now as his human legs began to change. The knees were reversing direction. His spine elongated into the beginnings of a tail.

That's when the screaming started.

"Ahhh ahhhhh!"

"What is it? What IS it?"

People were screaming and running and dropping their bags as they caught a glimpse of the nightmare creature Ax had become. Half-human, half-Andalite. A fluid, shifting mess of half-formed features.

I couldn't blame them. I felt like screaming myself.

We were getting near the exit, racing past the shoe repair place.

Suddenly, Ax fell forward, tangled up in his own mutating legs. He skidded on the polished marble floor.

Most of the crowd had been left behind, but the mall guards were still with us.

"You kids get out of the way!" one of them yelled at us. "This guy could be dangerous."

Ax sprang up. He was much more sure of himself, now that he was on his four Andalite hooves. The morph was almost entirely complete. His mouth was gone. His extra eyes were in place. His two arms and four legs were fully formed.

Then, at the very last, the tail appeared.

It was then that I heard the nearest guard, in an awed, frightened whisper, say, "Andalite!"

I quickly turned and looked at him. Only a Controller would recognize an Andalite.

The Controller guard drew his gun from his holster.

"RUN!" I yelled at Ax.

The Controller stood between Ax and the door. Big mistake. The Andalite tail flashed, faster than my eyes could follow. The guard's gun went flying through the air. He clutched at a hand that was red with blood.

Out the door we blew, running for our lives.

Sirens!

"Those are real cops coming," I said. "Not mall rent-a-cops!"

<Where should we go?> Ax demanded, reverting to thought-speak.

"Oh, *now* he wants advice?!" I looked around frantically. The bus was not really an option. The mall guards poured from the glass doors. The city police screamed towards us in their patrol cars.

All we could do was run. So we ran. Up rows of parked cars. Two kids and a guy who did not

belong on this planet.

"The grocery store!" Jake yelled.

"What?" I gasped. I was getting tired.

"In there!" he pointed. It was the grocery store across the parking lot. It was the only way we could go.

Police cars screeched to a halt all around us.

"Freeze!"

"I don't think so," I said.

We jetted through the big glass doors of the supermarket at a full, panicked run. I halfway expected to hear guns firing and bullets whizzing.

"Jake!" I yelled. "Help me here!" I had an idea for slowing down our pursuers. I grabbed a big row of parked grocery trolleys and shoved them back towards the doors. Jake grabbed on and helped.

Then we were off and running again, with Ax skittering shakily on the slippery floor and banging into groceries. Cans of olives and tomatoes crashed behind him.

Customers screamed and crashed their carts into each other.

"It's a monster! Mummy, it's a monster!" some little kid yelled.

"It's just a pretend monster," his mother said.

Yeah. A pretend monster. Right.

Then I saw our way out. It was at the end of the aisle. But I needed some time. I needed to get everyone out of our way. We couldn't have witnesses.

"There's a bomb!" I screamed, at the top of my lungs. "BOMB!"

"What?" Jake demanded.

"There's a bomb! A bomb in the shop! Run! Run! Everyone out! A BOMB!"

"What are you doing?!" Jake yelled.

"The cops have the place surrounded. There's only one way out," I snapped. I pointed.

I pointed at the live lobster tank at the end of the aisle by the seafood counter.

"Oh, no," Jake groaned.

"Oh, yes." I grinned.

The shoppers were running in panic, either from the supposed bomb or just from Ax. But the baskets in the doorway and the people shoving to escape slowed the cops down for a precious few moments.

I had a feeling the Controller cops were making sure that no real cops came in after us. They wanted us for themselves. And with no human witnesses.

"Let's go for a swim," I said.

It was a big lobster tank, fortunately. I hoisted myself up the side and climbed in. Jake was right behind me. We each grabbed a lobster and threw one to Ax.

It was not easy "acquiring" the lobster. It took

concentration. And all I could think was that there were an awful lot of cops outside the store, probably getting ready to rush in. And they would all have guns.

The lobster went limp and passive, the way animals do when you acquire them.

I dropped him back in the water. We stripped off our outer clothes and shoes and stuffed them, along with the Radio Shack bag, into a rubbish bin.

Ax had already begun to morph. Jake and I waited till he had shrunk a little and then hauled him into the tank with us.

He was already hard, like armour, and his arms had begun to split open and swell.

Then I began the morph.

I've been afraid a lot since we became Animorphs. But I have not got used to it. And I can tell you, I was so scared my bones were rattling.

At any second they were going to rush in.

At any moment they were going to catch us half-morphed.

I looked over at Jake. His own eyes were gone, replaced by little black ball-bearings.

"Ewww."

As I watched, eight spindly, blue, insect-like legs erupted from his chest.

"Aaaaahhh!" I yelped in shock.

Jake's face seemed to open up, to split open

into a complex mess of valves. I think I would have thrown up, seeing that. Except that I, also, no longer had a mouth.

At that very moment, I felt antennae explode from my forehead like impossibly long spears.

I was shrinking as I morphed, falling, falling, falling down into the water which had been around my thighs and was now around my neck.

I had the terrifying sensation of knowing that all the bones inside my body were dissolving, as a hard, fingernail-like crust covered me all over.

My human body was melting away.

My human vision was fading. I could no longer see the way a human sees.

Which was a good thing. Because I really did not want to see what I was becoming.

Chapter 7

I think I might have just started screaming and never stopped. But I no longer had a mouth, or throat, or vocal cords capable of making sounds.

But I had four sets of legs. I had two huge pincers. I could see them, kind of. They were a fractured image in my lobster eyes. I couldn't see much of the rest of me. But I could see other lobsters in the water.

I was very frightened.

Eat.

Eat.

Kill and eat.

The lobster brain surfaced suddenly, bubbling up within my human awareness. It had two thoughts.

Eat.

Eat.

Kill and eat.

I was now getting input from senses I couldn't begin to understand. My extraordinarily long antennae felt water temperature, and water current, and vibration. But I didn't know what any of it meant.

My eyes were almost useless at first. They showed fractured, incredible images, with none of the colours I knew.

I could see my pincers out in front of me. I could see my antennae. And behind me I could see a curved, brownish-blue surface, with humps and bumps on it.

My body! I realized with a sickening sensation. That was my back. My hard shell.

I could not look down and see my belly, or the hairy swimmerets scurrying away, back beneath my tail. I could not see my eight spider-like legs, but I could feel as they propelled me suddenly, scrabbling along the glass bottom of the tank.

<Jake?> I called out.

<Yeah. I'm here,> he said. He sounded shaky. Which was fine, because I was on the verge of crying. If lobsters could cry.

<You OK?>

<Yeah. This isn't my favourite morph, though.>

<No,> I agreed. It was good being able to

talk to him. I mean, you'd think you were losing your mind otherwise.

<Ax?> Jake called.

<I . . . I feel. . . I am hungry. This animal wants to eat,> Ax answered.

<Yeah, well, that's pretty normal for morphs,> I said. <Most animals care about food and not about much else. I don't think lobsters are exactly geniuses.>

<It wants to find prey,> Ax said wonderingly.

<I know. Who'd have figured lobsters were predators?> I said.

<It's easier to deal with a predator brain than with prey. That prey fear can be overwhelming,> Jake said.

I saw a lobster close by. <Is that you, Jake? Wiggle your left pincer.>

The left pincer did not move. I realized this lobster had a rubber band around his pincer. None of us had rubber bands. Rubber bands were not a part of the lobster DNA.

I saw a lobster to my left, unbanded. And another behind him. That was the three of us. There were half a dozen rubber-banded lobsters floating or just sitting.

<Speaking of fear,> I said. <Can anyone see out of the tank?>

<Just shadows,> Jake said. <These are pathetic eyes.>

<Yes, even worse than your human eyes,> Ax commented.

<This is really creepy,> I said. <I've never had an exoskeleton before.>

<These pincers are most excellent, though,> Ax said.

I saw him opening and closing them.

<Ax?> Jake said. <You say you can keep track of time accurately? Start tracking.>

<Yes, Prince Jake,> Ax said. <So far, ten of your minutes have passed.>

<That much?> I was surprised. <Ten minutes? The cops must have come in by now.>

<I was thinking the same thing,> Jake said.

<We better wait as long as we can. Close to the full two hours,> I said. <Although I really don't want to spend any more time than I have to in this creepy morph.>

According to Ax, an hour had passed when it happened.

I felt a strange disturbance in the water. Something large had splashed in. I sensed something above me.

Before I could think or react, I felt pressure on my shell.

I was rising rapidly through the water, being lifted.

<Jake! Something has me!>

Sudden shock!

I was out of the water.

Dryness. Heat. My antennae waved wildly as I tried to understand. My eyes registered nothing but bright light and huge, indistinct shadows.

Something large closed tightly over my right pincer. I could not open it. Then my left.

Rubber bands! I couldn't see them in this waterless environment. I was nearly blind. But I knew what had happened.

Someone had picked me up and rubber-banded my pincers.

Then I was tumbling, sliding, rubbing against things I could tell were other lobsters.

<Jake! Are you in this, too?>

<Yeah, but don't ask me what it means. I can't see or hear very well.>

<Is it them? Is it Controllers?>

Something very cold dropped on me and slithered around my body.

Ice?

I felt a sensation of swinging back and forth for a while, like being on a swing.

<Ax?>

<Yes, Marco. I am here, too. What is happening?>

<You got me,> I said. <Maybe the cops have us. Maybe the Controllers have us. I don't know.>

<Let's stay in morph as long as we can,>

Jake said. <Maybe we'll figure it out. But if it's the Controllers who have us, the last thing we want to do is demorph.>

The ice seemed to be making me sleepy. Or not exactly sleepy, just slow. Sluggish.

I guess I kind of zoned out for a while. I didn't know for how long, until I became suddenly alert and heard Ax's drowsy voice in my head saying, <We have only seven minutes left.>

That jolted me. I was not about to spend the rest of my life trapped as a lobster.

<OK, I am *out* of this morph, I don't care who sees,> I yelled.

<Agreed,> Jake said. <Time's up. We have to take our chances.>

<At least it's warmer now,> I said. I tried to look around, but my antennae felt nothing in the air. And my eyes only saw meaningless, blurry grey forms.

I focused on demorphing. I wondered if I could close my human eyes when Jake started to reappear. I really did not want to watch Jake and Ax demorph. Once was enough. I would already have nightmares for a month.

<Here goes,> I said. I began the change.

But just then I again felt the sensation of pressure on my shell. My pincers came free. Someone, or something, had removed the rubber bands.

And suddenly I felt a warmth billowing up around me.

Steam.

<Oh, no.>

Chapter 8

<NOOOOOO!>I screamed silently.

I knew where I was! I was in someone's hand, about to be dropped into a pot of boiling water.

<NOOOOOOOOO!>

And maybe it was because I was so desperate to scream, or maybe it was just the luck of the morph, but my human mouth was one of the first things to emerge.

Small, open lips appeared in place of my lobster mouth.

I didn't have normal lungs or vocal cords yet, so I couldn't make a sound.

But I guess I didn't have to.

I guess suddenly having lips appear on a lobster was enough to make the woman drop me.

I fell. My front pincers caught the edge of the pan. Sheer dumb luck. I hung onto the edge of the pan as my tail curled up, centimetres above the boiling water in the pot.

I grew rapidly, becoming a baby-sized creature half-covered with hard cuticle, half flesh. Human eyes grew in place of the useless stalk eyes. The antennae sucked back into my forehead. I heard a familiar grinding sound as my spine reappeared inside me.

With a desperate surge of energy, I tumbled over the side of the pan and landed flat on my shell back, on top of the stove. I was looking up into a stove hood.

I rolled away from the heat and fell.

But the fall wasn't far, because I was now the size of a toddler, more human than lobster. I was one nasty-looking kid, though, with eight legs growing from my stomach and chest.

My human hearing suddenly returned with shocking effect.

"Ahhhhhh! Ahhhhhhh! Ahhhhhh! Ahhhhhhh! Ahhhhhhh!"

Someone was screaming uncontrollably.

My legs were back! I stood up. I looked around and saw a woman. Sort of pretty, except for the fact that her eyes were wide with terror and she was screaming.

"Ahhhhhhhh! Ahhhhhhhhh! Ahhhhhhhh!"

I glanced over and saw the plastic bag filled with ice. That's how she had carried us from the supermarket. Now we were in her kitchen. Jake was already mostly human, standing with one foot still in the shopping bag. The eight legs sucked into his chest. His human eyes appeared.

Ax was a disgusting combination of Andalite and lobster. But as I watched, he eliminated the last traces of crustacean.

Unfortunately, this did not make the woman feel any better.

"Ahhhhhhhhh! Ahhhhhhhhhh! Ahhhhhhhh!"

"It's OK, ma'am," I said. "We're not going to hurt you."

"Calm down, ma'am," Jake said. "Please calm down."

Her eyes darted wildly from me to Jake to Ax. She kept screaming.

"Ahhhhhhhhh! Ahhhhhhhhh! Ahhhhhhh!"

"Look, it's OK," I said. "We're going to leave. No one is going to hurt you."

"You . . . you . . . you . . . you . . . lobsters!" she managed to say.

"Yeah, it is slightly weird, I'll admit," I said. "But it's OK. It's just a dream."

"A . . . a . . . a dream?"

"Yes, ma'am. It's just a dream," Jake said as reassuringly as he could.

I looked at Ax. "Can you morph to human yet? We need to get out of here."

"I can morph again," he assured me. And he started right away.

"We're going to leave now," Jake said. "You can wake up later, OK? But I wouldn't tell anyone about this dream."

The woman shook her head violently.

"See, it could get you in trouble with . . . with certain people. Besides, folks would just think you're crazy."

She nodded with extreme conviction.

Ax was almost human. We were all dressed in our slightly ridiculous morphing outfits, but they would have to do.

We headed for the door. Then I caught sight of three more lobsters, still in the bag of ice. I guess it was supposed to be a dinner for six.

"Ma'am?" I asked. "Do us a favour, would you, please? Take those other guys down to the beach and let them go. OK?"

Chapter 9

Jake and I were playing video games at the mall. I was beating him easily. He was distracted because he was eating.

He was eating a big red bug with huge pincers.

I told him not to eat it. It would upset his stomach. But he just ignored me.

Then, suddenly, his stomach exploded. It just exploded outward, guts flying everywhere. Eight huge spider legs appeared, like something in him was trying to crawl out.

I tried to get away, but the steam was rising. I was burning up!

I tried to run, but my legs were gone, replaced by a tail that jerked and kicked.

I screamed.

And screamed.

"Marco, Marco, wake up!"

My eyes opened very suddenly. Darkness. Someone holding on to me. I was confused.

"Mum?" I asked.

Silence. Then, "No."

My brain snapped back into reality. I was in my room. In my own bed. My dad was sitting on the side of the bed. He looked concerned and sad.

"It's just me," he said quietly. He let go of my shoulders.

I felt sweaty all over. Cold sweat.

"I guess you had a nightmare," my father said.

"Yeah," I said shakily. "Sorry I woke you up."

"I wasn't asleep," he said.

I glanced at my clock. The red numbers showed 3:18 A.M. I didn't have to ask why my dad was awake. He often sat awake late into the night. Sometimes watching TV. Sometimes just staring into space.

He'd been that way since my mum died.

My dad looks very different from me. For one thing, he's pretty tall. He's paler than me, too, and has light brown eyes. My mum was Hispanic, very dark hair and eyes. Everyone says I look like her. I know it's true, because sometimes when he's thinking about her, my dad will just glaze over and stare at me like I'm not even there. Like I'm a picture of someone else.

"I'm OK now," I said. "You should try to get some sleep."

He nodded. "Yeah. I'll do that. Look, Marco, you weren't dreaming about *her,* were you?"

"No, Dad. Why?"

"Because the first thing you said when you woke up was 'Mum.'"

"I guess I was confused."

"Do you ever? Dream about her, I mean?"

"Sometimes," I admitted. "But they aren't nightmares."

He almost smiled. "No. I guess they wouldn't be, would they?" He picked up the little framed picture of my mum that I keep on my nightstand. Then he got that twisted look of sick grief I had seen on his face every day for the last two years.

Part of me is mad when I see him that way. Part of me just wants to say, "Dad, get it together. Let her go. She's dead. She doesn't want us spending the rest of our lives mourning."

But I never do say that.

After a few minutes, he got up. He made some last remark about how I shouldn't be worried about bogeymen, and left. I knew he would sit out in the living room alone, and eventually fall asleep in his chair.

I lay there in the dark and tried to get the dream out of my head. But it's hard to forget a nightmare that's true.

<There. It is finished.> Ax held up a small mess of electronic components for all of us to see. It looked sort of like an exploded remote control, but smaller.

It was the next day. We were out in the woods, grouped together beneath a huge old oak tree. It was like a strange sort of picnic. Jake and Cassie had each brought hand tools for Ax to use — screwdrivers, a solder gun, a battery-powered drill, a hammer, wrenches, pliers and, of course we had the electronic parts we had stashed in the rubbish before the lobster incident.

Rachel had brought sandwiches. I'd brought a six-pack of Pepsi.

It was a nice day, sunny and warm. I needed a nice day. I needed sunlight. I'd had a bad night, with too little sleep.

"So, Ax," I said. "What is it?"

<It is a distress beacon that can broadcast on Yeerk frequencies,> he said with satisfaction. <I know this is a Yeerk frequency. We have used it to trick them before. To send false instructions.>

"All it needs is a Z-Space transponder," Jake said wearily, rolling his eyes at me.

I think Jake may have been a bit ragged out

by the lobster incident, too. He seemed snappish and kind of unfocused. Not at all Jake-like.

"And since we can't get a Z-Space transponder, it's basically useless, right?" Rachel asked.

<Yes. Totally useless without the transponder.>

Rachel threw up her hands. "Then exactly what are we doing?"

Jake just shrugged. Cassie sidled up next to him and gave him a small little sideways hug. No one was supposed to notice. But right away Jake's harsh look mellowed a little.

That wasn't doing anything for *my* bad mood, though. "Well, I'm guessing that in about two centuries or so, humans will discover zero space and make transponders. Whatever *they* are. But in the meantime, I'm going to have a sandwich."

Tobias came drifting down through the branches and leaves of the tree, almost silent. He landed on a low branch of the oak. <No one anywhere near here,> he reported. <Looks safe. At least as far as you guys are concerned. But there's a golden eagle about a kilometre south. I think I'll stay out of sight for a while and hope he goes away.>

Not for the first time, I realized just how tough Tobias's life is. He shares the same dangers we do, but he also has all the dangers that come from being a red-tail hawk. Golden

eagles sometimes prey on hawks. They are bigger and faster than he is.

<So. What's up?> Tobias asked.

"We have a completely useless distress beacon," Rachel said. "We need a transponder that probably won't be invented on this planet for a century or two."

<How about Chapman?> Tobias said.

"What about Chapman?" I asked. Chapman is the assistant principal at our school. He's also one of the most important Controllers.

I used to hate Chapman. I mean, once I knew that he was a Controller and all. But then we learned that he surrendered his freedom to the Yeerks as part of a deal to keep his daughter, Melissa, safe.

It's hard to hate someone for protecting their kid. Even if he or she ended up being a deadly enemy. That's one of the terrible things about fighting the Yeerks. The real enemy is just the evil slug in a person's brain. The host is usually totally innocent.

<We know that Chapman communicates with Visser Three,> Tobias said. <He talks to Visser Three on the Yeerk mother ship, or on the Blade ship. Wherever Visser Three is. Doesn't that mean that Chapman's secret radio thing must have one of these Z-Space transponders?>

<Yes!> Ax said instantly. <If this Controller

speaks to any Yeerk ship, he would have to have a Z-Space transponder. The Yeerk ships are all cloaked. Cloaking technology requires a Z-Space deflection.>

Jake caught my eye. "That's pretty much what I figured."

I smiled, despite the fact that I had a bad feeling about the way that this conversation was going.

"How big is a Z-Space thingie?" Cassie asked.

Ax held two of his fingers close together, indicating something the size of a pea. <There would be several redundant units in any transmitter. We could take one without it being noticed. At least not right away.>

Rachel stood. "We are not going into Chapman's house again," she said firmly. "The last time we did, we almost got Melissa made into a Controller. We cannot morph her cat again. Chapman is on guard now. It won't be easy this time." She realized what she'd said and added, "Not that it was exactly easy the first time."

"A historic first," I observed. "Rachel saying 'no' to a mission."

"Rachel's right," Jake said. "We do *nothing* that will endanger Melissa again. So the cat is out. Also any other plan that means major risk that Chapman will discover us."

For a while no one said anything.

Finally Ax spoke silently in our heads. <I cannot ask anyone to take risks for me. You rescued me from the bottom of the ocean. You sheltered me. And my foolishness almost got Prince Jake and Marco killed yesterday.>

What he said surprised me a little. I guess I'd expected him to argue that we should try and help him.

"What if . . ." Cassie began.

We all looked at her. "Yes?" Jake asked.

"What if there was a way to get into Chapman's basement room — the secret room where he keeps the transmitter — without even going through the house? With almost no chance of getting caught?"

I felt my heart sink. "As long as it doesn't involve anything with an exoskeleton."

I'd meant it as a joke. But Cassie just looked at me solemnly.

"What?" I demanded. "A lobster again? How is a lobster —"

"No," she said. "Think smaller. Much smaller. Much, much smaller."

Chapter 10

Ants. That was Cassie's brilliant idea. Ants.

See, ants could easily get into Chapman's basement. And ants could carry away the small transponder.

Ants.

This was what my life had come to. We ended up spending a couple of hours debating whether we should be red ants or black ants. I finally left in disgust. I didn't want to be an ant, red, black, or any other colour.

I saw Jake the next day in school. I had just come out of history class, where I had blown a simple test.

I wasn't in the best mood.

I was opening my locker and muttering about

the Mexican-American War, and how was anyone supposed to remember the difference between that war and the Texas war of independence.

"Hi," Jake said. "The answer is black. Turns out most of the ants near Chapman's house are black. Tobias checked it out."

I looked over Jake's shoulder to make sure no one was close enough to overhear. "Jake, I don't want to be an insect. I've been a gorilla, an osprey, a wolf, a dolphin, a seagull, a trout, a lobster . . . and I'm probably forgetting a few. Gorilla was fun. Dolphin was fun. Osprey was fun. Ant? Not fun. Basically, insects are a bad idea."

Jake shrugged. "I was a flea. That was no big thing." He grinned like he'd made the world's funniest joke. "Seriously, it was like nothing. I couldn't see anything. I could barely hear anything, just vibrations. All I knew was I liked warm bodies and whenever I got hungry I just poked a hole in some warm skin."

"And sucked blood."

He looked a little uncomfortable. "Well, it was Rachel's blood. Kind of. I mean, OK, it was cat blood, but Rachel was morphing the cat."

"Jake? Do you ever listen to yourself?"

"I try not to think about it," he admitted. "But look, we want to try and give Ax a chance to get home. And if he stays here he's a danger to us. We've got this big Anda —" He looked around to make sure no one could hear, and lowered his voice. "We have this big Andalite running around Cassie's farm. What if someone sees him? Any Controller is going to know what he is. And they're going to wonder why he's on Cassie's land."

I nodded. "Yeah. You're right. But I almost died the other day. I was almost boiled alive. I know you're the big hero type, Jake, but I'm not."

I grabbed my book out of the locker, slammed the door, and headed down the hall. Jake kept pace.

"You know what next Sunday is?" I asked him suddenly. I hadn't planned to say anything.

"Sunday? I don't know. What?"

"Two years, to the day. Two years since my mum died. And I don't know what to do. I don't know whether I should talk to my dad about it, or just let it pass. But I know one thing — this would be a really bad week for me to turn up dead."

I kept walking. He didn't follow me.

Two years.

She'd taken the boat out of the marina. She'd sailed it out into a rough sea. No one knew why. She'd never done it before. We'd always gone out together, the three of us.

That night, after the high winds had blown past, they found the boat driven up on to the

rocks. The hull was shattered. There was no sign of my mother, except for a frayed safety rope.

They never found her body. The Coast Guard guys said that was not unusual. The ocean is a big place.

So is space, a voice in my head said.

Somewhere, very, very far away, a mother and father wondered what had become of their children.

For a long time, I made up stories about how my mum had survived. Maybe on a desert island or something. But I'm a realistic person, I guess. After a while I accepted it.

And after a while, Ax's parents would accept that he and his brother, Prince Elfangor, would not be returning. That they had been lost forever in space.

Lost fighting to protect Earth. Trying to help the human race.

To help me.

I spotted Cassie up ahead, walking with some of her friends. She smiled vaguely when she saw me. We were supposed to kind of ignore each other in school, so no one would ever figure out that Jake and me and Cassie and Rachel were hanging out a lot.

As I brushed past her I muttered, "Tell Jake I'll do it."

Sometimes I really hate having a conscience.

Chapter 11

"I wonder why these people moved?" Cassie said.

"Maybe they didn't like living next door to a Controller who is part of a conspiracy to take over the world," I said. "Or else maybe they just don't like assistant principals. I could understand that."

We were standing in the backyard of the house next to Chapman's. It was empty. There was a "For Sale" sign in the front yard. It did make you kind of wonder why these people had decided to move. Not that Chapman ever acted strange. That's the big problem with Controllers — you can never tell who is or who isn't.

"It's convenient for us, anyway," Jake said.

It was night. The moon was high and full and bright, so we were hiding beneath a tree. There

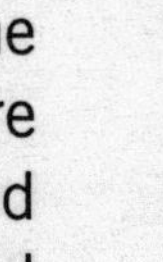

was a high wooden fence between us and Chapman's.

Ax was just changing from his human morph back into his Andalite body.

We had already acquired some ants earlier, at Cassie's barn. We were getting ready to do it. I was scared. Badly scared.

I guess the others were, too. Everyone was talking too much, the way you do when you're nervous. Cassie was shivering like she was cold, only it was about seventy degrees out.

"Tobias?" I asked. He was in the tree, just a few inches over my head on a low branch. "How well can you see?"

<I think I'll be able to see you as long as you stay above ground,> he said. <The moonlight helps. But I'm not nearly as good at night as I am during the day. My eyes aren't much better than yours in the dark.>

"Swell," I said.

Jake glanced at his watch. "It's time. We know Chapman will be at the meeting of The Sharing, starting about now."

The Sharing is a "front" organization for Controllers. It's a way for Controllers to get together without anyone being suspicious. Supposedly, it's just a sort of combined Boy Scouts and Girl Scouts. In reality it's a way for the Controllers to recruit willing hosts.

Yes, believe it or not, some people *choose* to accept Yeerk control.

We didn't have to ask how Jake knew about the meeting of The Sharing. Jake's brother, Tom, is one of them. A Controller who is very into The Sharing.

"You ready, Ax?" Jake asked. The Andalite had to be back in Andalite form before he could morph. Just like all of us had to be human before morphing into another being. Once Cassie had tried morphing straight from one animal to another. Nothing had happened. And Cassie is the best morpher.

<I am ready,> Ax said.

"Everyone ready?" Jake asked.

"Yep," Rachel said.

Even she sounded tense. There was a bad feeling hanging over this whole thing. Or maybe I was just being paranoid.

"OK," Jake said. "Soon as we're all morphed, we head across the grass, down along the wall, underground. We find a crack or a hole, and enter the basement."

"Yeah. Nothing to it," I said.

I concentrated hard on the ant I had acquired earlier. There wasn't much to think about, really. When I'd held the ant in my hand it had just been this tiny little dot. You could see that it had a sectioned body and legs, but that was about it.

The morphing began very quickly.

"Whoa!"

Falling! Falling!

That was the first sensation. I was shrinking rapidly. The ground was rushing up at me. It was like one of those nightmares where you are falling and falling but never seem to hit the ground.

I was still maybe half a metre tall when my skin seemed to turn crisp, as if it had been burned. It became hard. Harder than fingernails and glossy black.

I looked over at Cassie and nearly screamed.

She was farther along than me. Only thirty centimetres tall and hard-shelled black all over. Glistening, ridged, plastic-looking skin.

Her legs were shrivelling rapidly. So were her arms, although they had become longer, to match her legs.

The third set of legs was growing out of her chest.

And her face . . .

Her face was no longer human. Her head was turning sort of teardrop-shaped. Wickedly-curved mandibles were growing out of her mouth — huge, slashing, deadly-looking serrated jaws.

Her eyes had gone flat and dead. Just black dots. Antennae, looking almost like another set of legs, sprouted from her forehead.

Her waist was pinched tight. Her lower body

swelled till it looked as big as a watermelon.

I didn't want to watch. Because I knew that all these same changes were happening to me. I knew it. I didn't want to think about it. I just wanted it to be over. I wanted the changes to be done.

Suddenly, all around me, huge, raspy spears shot up out of the ground!

Grass! I was diminishing to true insect size. The rough, sharp shafts that were rising all around me were just blades of grass. They weren't growing. I was shrinking.

One exploded directly under me. I tumbled, end over end.

And then my eyesight failed. My eyes simply stopped functioning.

I was blind!

Blind, and falling, rolling, cartwheeling down the side of a blade of grass.

Chapter 12

I was standing upright. I knew that. I had stopped falling.

But I was blind.

No, not completely blind. It was not just blackness. But my eyes saw no detail. I could see patches of light and areas of darkness. But they were misty and fragmented, and my ant brain was not interested in them.

No. The world was not about sight any more.

It was all . . . something else. I knew I was getting something. Something . . . a sense. A feeling, almost.

Then, I could feel . . . I could feel my antennae waving. Waving back and forth, searching. Searching . . . no. They were *smelling.*

My antennae were smelling. I was looking for a scent. Several scents. It was not like human smell. Not like Jake had described dog scent when he'd morphed his dog Homer.

That kind of scent is full of possibilities. And subtleties.

This was different. I was looking for just a few scents. Just a few smells.

I tried to prepare myself. I had been through this before. There is usually a time, a brief few seconds, before the animal mind appears with all its fear and hunger and intensity. I needed to be prepared. Ants were tiny and weak. Surely their fear would be extreme. I would have to be —

Then, wham!

The ant's mind erupted inside my own!

There was no fear. None.

There was no hunger.

There was no . . . no *self.* No *me.*

No me.

No . . .

My antennae swept the air. Strange. Not home. Not the colony.

Enemy territory.

Smell them. Smell their droppings. Smell the acrid odours they smeared along the ground to mark their boundaries.

<How are you guys doing? It's Tobias. How are you guys doing?>

Strangers. The smell of others. They would come. There would be killing.

Killing. Soon.

Move.

<Jake. Marco. Rachel. Cassie. Answer me. It's Tobias. Talk to me.>

I began moving. My six legs picked their way nimbly. I was a nearly blind insect, picking his way through a forest of giant saw-edged grass blades.

Food. The smell of food. Find it. Take it. Return to the colony with it.

Change direction instantly. Move towards the smell of dead beetle. Others around. Us. Ours. They had the right smell. They were not enemy.

<You guys are heading the wrong way.>

Moving faster now. Feet feeling each blade of grass. Antennae sweeping the air, searching for the scent of the enemy. Searching for the scent of the dead carcass that we had to find and return to the colony.

<Listen to me! You are going the wrong way! The ant minds are controlling you!>

Close now. The scent of food was stronger.

Mandibles working. We would touch the carcass. We would judge its size. If it was too big to carry, we would hack it into smaller pieces and carry the chunks to the colony.

<You have to take control! You have to fight! You have to get a grip!>

Or enemies would come. And kill.

The smell of enemies was everywhere.

There. We had reached the dead beetle. I scented the air. I touched it with my legs, touching again and again to learn the size.

I? *My* legs?

Confusion.

<Fight! Fight it! You have to get control!>

It was big.

The others were with me. I opened my cutting mandibles wide and bit into the beetle, slicing tough shell, biting into meat.

<Listen to me. You are losing. You have to fight!>

Fight?

Suddenly, I realized that there had been something . . . a sound. Yes, not a smell. Not a smell. Not a feel.

<You are humans! You are *humans*! Listen to me. You are not ants. Fight it! *Fight it!*>

Yes, not a smell or a feel. In my head.

My.

Me.

Marco.

<AHHH!> I screamed inside my own head. Tobias said later that it scared him half to death. He thought I was being killed.

That wasn't it at all. I had been reborn.

<AHHHH! AHHHH! AHHHHH!>

<What's the matter?> Tobias cried.

<I . . . I . . . I lost myself,> I said. <I was gone. I was lost. I didn't even *exist.*>

<Get out of that morph!> Tobias said.

But I could hear the others now, snapping back into reality. Becoming again. Crying.

<What kind of creatures are these?> It was Ax. He sounded terrified. *Terrified.* <They have no self! I was lost! There was nothing to hold on to. They are not *whole.* They are only parts, like cells. Just pieces. What kind of foul creatures are these?>

<Listen. You guys morph back,> Tobias said. <This sucks. This isn't right.>

<Hive,> Cassie said, sounding shattered. <They are social insects. Part of a colony. A hive. I should have guessed. I should have *known.* Ax is right. Each of us is only a part. Like a single cell within a human body.>

<Guys? I see other ants. They're coming your way,> Tobias said.

<How far away?> Jake asked. <Can you see them up there?>

<I'm not in the tree. I'm right here. I'm standing right over you. You're only a few centimetres from my right talon.>

<I don't want to have to do this all over,>

Rachel said. <Let's do this. Let's get it *done.*>

<Are we all in control now?> Jake asked.

One by one, we said yes. It was only partly true. Yes, I had gained control over the ant mind. But it was still there. It was powerful in a totally new way. It was the simplicity that made it hard. The ant was a piece of a computer. Just a tiny switch, a part of a much bigger creature — the colony.

<Guys?> Cassie's "voice" in my head. <If you try, you can kind of use these ant eyes — a little, anyway. If you concentrate you can notice light and dark. It's like watching a really, really bad black-and-white TV that's almost all snow. And you can only see what's right in front of you. But you can almost see a picture.>

She was right. I could kind of see. But nothing I saw made any sense, anyway. I could recognize blades of grass. But a long, sloped wall that seemed about two metres high was a mystery to me.

<Someone just ran over my talon,> Tobias said.

The wall. Tobias's talon.

<That's good. You're heading in the right direction,> Tobias said. <You're coming up on the fence.>

If there was a fence, you couldn't prove it by me. I saw nothing. The bottom of the fence

was seven or eight body lengths above me. Irrelevant.

<I can't go into Chapman's yard,> Tobias said. <It would look fishy if anyone saw. Just keep going in the same direction.>

We did. I barrelled through a forest of grass. Then, very suddenly, it ended. We were out of the grass and racing across a bleak moonscape of boulders, each the size of my head.

In my ant brain the alarm bells were still ringing loudly. Enemies! Enemies! Their scent was everywhere.

But it was not fear I felt from the ant brain. It was not capable of emotion, or anything like emotion. It simply knew that there were enemies close by.

And it knew that it would come down, sooner or later, to kill, or be killed.

Chapter 13

We hit the wall. I knew it was the concrete wall of the foundation. I knew, logically, that just half a metre or so over my head, the wall became wood siding. But I could not see anything like that kind of distance.

What I saw and felt and "smelled" was that the horizontal world had simply stopped. Reality had a corner. The entire world, as far as I was concerned, was a corner between concrete and sand, one vertical, one horizontal. The concrete was full of cracks and pits big enough for me to climb inside of.

<Head down,> Jake reminded us. <Look for a way to follow the wall down.>

<There's a tunnel here,> Rachel said. <But

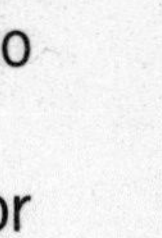

it . . . smells . . . bad. Real bad.>

She was right. I found the tunnel, too. It was one of *theirs.* It belonged to the enemy.

<I know there is an enemy. I can sense it,> Ax said. <But who? What?>

<I don't know,> Jake said grimly. <Let's just hope they're not around.>

We headed down the tunnel. The smell of the enemy was powerful. Their stench wrapped around us. We were an invading force. We were going deep, deep into enemy territory.

The tunnel was narrow. Boulders brushed constantly against my abdomen. My legs kicked some away. Others had to be moved aside. I should have felt cramped and claustrophobic, with the earth all around me, and my friends close ahead and behind me. But my ant mind was at home in tunnels.

I was travelling down. I knew my head was pointed down, but gravity seemed less important than it did when I was human.

<There's a side tunnel up here,> Rachel said. She was in the lead. Big surprise. <There are a couple of side tunnels. It's starting to branch out. Should I YAHHHH!>

<What? What?>

<Oh, oh, oh. An ant!>

<What? Rachel!>

<He's running! He's running away. It's OK.

It's OK. He was smaller than me. He ran off down a side tunnel.>

<I guess we're the baddest ants in the tunnel,> I said, trying to joke away the sudden clutch of very human terror.

<Let's hope so,> Jake said.

<I feel air,> Ax reported. <A breeze. Down this next side tunnel.>

<Follow it,> Jake said.

Quickly we were out of the sand boulders and into a canyon. That's what the gap seemed like, anyway. Like a deep, deep canyon. A crack in the concrete foundation.

We clambered over craggy rocks and squeezed along the narrow crack. All the while the breeze grew stronger.

Then we were out of the canyon. We were on a flat, vertical plane.

<I think we're there,> Cassie suggested. <I sense open space all around. Air. And it's dark.>

<OK. Morph out. But be careful.>

<Wait! Get horizontal first,> I said. <Humans can't cling to walls, and we don't know how high up we are.>

<Marco's right. And someone should go first.>

<For once, I volunteer,> I said. I couldn't wait to get out of that ant body.

First I moved away from them. It was totally

dark, so I didn't have to watch the changes in myself. But trust me, feeling them was bad enough.

Once I was human again, I began to look for a light. Then I froze.

My huge, human feet could crush my friends!

I stood perfectly still and ran my hands along the wall. Nothing. Nothing. A bulletin board. A desk! Phone. Some kind of machine, probably a fax. There! A lamp!

The sudden light was blinding. I blinked and covered my eyes with my hand. As soon as I could see, I looked around. I was in a very small room, like a windowless office. I was alone.

Then I looked down at my body. Arms. Legs. Feet. Yes! Human! Completely human.

<We see light,> Jake said. <I know you can't thought-speak now, so, if it's safe, flick the light.>

I could see them now. Four tiny ants, huddled against the corner of the wall. It took my breath away.

Had that been me? I had been one of them? Down there?

I flicked the light. Seconds later, they began to demorph. I turned away, and focused on rifling the desk.

"That was gross beyond belief," Cassie said. She was the first to complete her change.

"Yeah," I agreed.

"I don't want to do that again," she said. I could hear the shiver of fear and disgust in her voice.

I didn't answer. I was too scared to want to talk about it. If I talked about it, it would become real, you know? Better not to think. Better to shove it out of my mind.

"This is the place," Rachel said when she had grown eyes and a mouth again. "I recognize it. Chapman's office. I was a cat when I was in here, but this is it."

"Let's get this done. In and out," Jake said nervously. "Ax? Find that transponder."

Ax, now fully Andalite again, immediately began removing a panel from the thing I thought was a fax machine.

I continued looking through Chapman's desk. Nothing much there. No papers. No files.

Ax looked at me and smiled in that way Andalites have of smiling with just their eyes. He touched a small cube I thought was a paperweight. The paperweight lit up and projected a picture into the air in front of me.

"Cool," I said. "A computer, right?"

<Yes. A computer.>

I poked the air, pointing at a symbol that looked like it would be a folder. It opened. The document was written in some alien alphabet.

<You can use a computer?>

"Sure. Why not? This is a few hundred years more advanced than ours but —"

<Stop!> Ax said suddenly. <Go back to that last document.>

"You can read this stuff?"

<Yes.> He stared intently. <It is an announcement. The Yeerks will have an important visitor arriving soon. Visser One.>

"Visser One? That would be like Visser Three's boss?"

<Yes. Visser One is more powerful than Visser Three. Just as Visser Three is more powerful than Visser Four. There are forty-seven Vissers in the Yeerk empire. Or so we believe.>

"Great," I said. "Forty-seven. Not all like our friend Visser Three, I hope."

Ax was back at work getting the transponder out of the fax-like machine. <No,> he answered. <Only Visser Three has an Andalite body. Only he can morph. Visser One has a *human* body, I believe. Ah. Here, I have it.>

He held up a tiny, shiny disk. No bigger than a pea.

"OK, let's get out of here," Jake said. "Put that thing near the crack. We won't have to carry it as far. Everyone, morph back. Let's bale out."

It was the moment I dreaded. I didn't want to return to that ant body. It made me want to cry, just thinking of it. But there was no other way. If we tried to sneak out of the basement by going up through the house, we might be caught.

"Boy, I don't want to do this," I muttered. But at the same time, I focused on that ant shape. And as I watched, my friends began to change.

Once we had shrunk back to ant size, the transponder seemed enormous. It was far bigger than we were. Standing beside it, feeling it with my legs and antennae, it felt about as big as a two-car garage.

<Everybody says ants are incredibly strong for their size,> Cassie pointed out. <Let's see if that's true.>

It seemed impossible, but Cassie, Rachel and Ax managed to lift that monstrous load off the ground.

I mean, it was like seeing three people walking down the street carrying a city bus. That's how big it was. But it's true what they say about ants. For their size, they are some strong little bugs.

When we reached the vertical wall, the three of them had to push it ahead and roll it up the wall, like some gigantic steel doughnut.

We reached the crack. They pushed and shoved the transponder in. Jake and I were in the lead.

It took all five of us to drag that thing over the crags of the concrete canyon. But we made

it through and back to the dirt tunnel. The transponder was so big it blocked the tunnel. It was like a spitwad in a straw. But with Ax, Rachel and Cassie behind pushing, and Jake and I clearing boulders — grains of sand — out of the way, we made progress.

It happened suddenly.

There was no warning.

One second the tunnel ahead of me was empty. The next second it was full.

Full of a charging, racing army of ants.

Enemies, my ant brain said.

Now the killing would begin.

Chapter 14

<They're behind us!> It was Rachel, yelling.

<Breaking through the side of the tunnel!> Cassie screamed.

<They're everywhere!>

<Help! Help!>

<Arrrrgggghhhh!>

The speed of the attack was incredible. The force of the attack was impossible to explain. There were hundreds of them. Ahead. Behind. Flooding up from side tunnels. Bursting from the walls.

<My leg! They bit off my leg!>

<Oh, oh, oh! My neck. Oh, help me!>

There were three of them on me. They were pulling me, trying to force me down so they could

tear me apart.

Tear me apart!

A fourth scampered over my head, brushing my antennae. He locked his mandibles on my narrow waist. He was trying to bite me in half.

There was no defence. We could not win. We would all be dead in a few seconds.

They were machines. Absolutely without fear. Unstoppable.

<Morph!> I yelled. <It's the only way! Morph!>

One of my legs came loose, torn away. Ripped out by the roots.

<Aaarrrgghhh!>

<No! No! Help me!>

I could feel my waist being sawed through by grinding sharp mandibles.

A searing liquid was fired at me. Poison. They were stinging me. Stinging me again and again, and ripping me apart.

Human. I wanted to be human again. Please, just let me live long enough to become human again!

<Morph!> Jake's voice. Then, <Aaaaahhhhh! No! NO!>

My waist would snap. The mandibles would not release me.

Then, suddenly, the pressure around my waist was gone. Instead, I felt the sandy soil pressing against me.

I was growing!

I couldn't breathe. Sand blocked the air. Pressure. Then, the ground around me opened up. I swear it was like climbing up out of a grave. The air! Fresh, clean night air!

I exploded up out of the sand.

Jake was on top of me, pushing against me as he grew. And the others, who had been only inches away in the tunnel, also pressed together in a rapidly growing heap of misshapen bodies. I tried to squirm away, but it was awkward. I was only half human.

But at last I lay there on the ground, staring up through human eyes at the stars.

<Are you guys OK?> It was Tobias.

"Cassie?" Jake asked.

"I'm OK," Cassie said.

"Me, too, Jake, thanks for asking," Rachel said.

We were all alive. All in one piece. Four humans and an Andalite.

I looked down and saw the disturbed sand, where we had pushed our way up and out. Racing wildly about were thousands of ants, almost too small to see.

There, too, in the dirt, was the transponder. I picked it up.

Rachel was stamping the ground back down, trying to flatten it out so it wouldn't look strange.

"Jake?" I said. "Let's not do this again any time soon."

He nodded shakily.

"One day I'm a lobster. The next I'm an ant. I figure the next step down the evolutionary ladder is a virus or something. And I just want to say right now, I'm not doing it. I am not going to become phlegm, even to save the world."

It wasn't much of a joke, but there was a kind of lame little laugh from everyone. And Rachel stopped stamping on the ants — I mean, the ground.

That night, when I went home, I took a shower. I found the head of an ant. It was still locked on to the skin of my waist.

Lots of people think only humans fight wars. That only humans are murderous. Let me tell you something — compared to ants, human beings are full of nothing but peace, love and understanding.

A month or so after the experience with the ants, I picked up a book about ants. The author said, "If ants had nuclear weapons they would probably end the world in a week."

He's wrong. It wouldn't take them that long.

Chapter 15

I was cool. I was fine. I slept OK. There were dreams, but I just put them out of my mind.

When I got up the next morning, I ignored the fact that my dad's eyes were red, like he'd been crying. He was getting worse, not better, as we got closer to Sunday. To the second anniversary of my mum's death.

But I had to put that out of my mind, too. I had to put a lot of things out of my mind. It was getting to be a habit.

I saw Jake in the hallway at school. I pretended not to notice him.

I saw Rachel, too. She had a dark look in her eyes. Like she hadn't slept. Like something was *really* wrong.

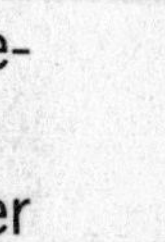

Even Cassie seemed grim. It had got to all of us. It's not so easy to just forget terror. It's not easy to just ignore the memory of your leg being ripped off.

Of being dismembered. Torn apart.

One of these days, I thought, one of us is going to go crazy. Totally, lock-me-up-in-a-rubber-room nuts. It was too much. This wasn't how life was supposed to be.

One of us would snap. One of us would lose it. It could happen, even to strong people.

I knew. It had happened to my father. I used to think nothing could ever destroy him. But my mum's death had.

He used to be an engineer. A scientist, really. He's incredibly smart. We had a nice house. We had a nice car. I used to live practically next door to Jake.

I know all that stuff isn't important. I know having things isn't what life is about. But it was still hard when my dad just stopped going to work. Jerry, his boss, tried to be nice. He gave him a couple of weeks to deal with losing Mum.

But a couple of weeks was not enough.

My dad's a janitor now. Part-time. He gets jobs through a temping agency. He unpacks boxes at department stores. That kind of thing. But I don't care what kind of job he has. That doesn't matter.

What matters is that when I lost my mum, I lost my dad, too.

See, people can snap. People can lose it. I know.

I cruised through the morning classes. No big deal.

At lunch I ended up at a table with Rachel. She didn't seem to notice me. She was just hunched over her meal, eating mechanically.

A girl named Jessica came walking past with her tray. She bumped into Rachel, which made Rachel drop her fork. It splattered down in the food on her tray.

I don't know if Jessica did it deliberately or not. She's the kind of girl who thinks she's tough.

"Watch it!" Rachel snapped.

"What?" Jessica demanded, acting outraged. "Are you yelling at me? Don't give me any of your mouth, I might have to slap it for you." Then she shoved against Rachel's back.

In a flash Rachel was up, out of her seat. She spun around. She grabbed Jessica by the collar of her sweatshirt and pushed the girl back against the next table.

Jessica probably outweighs Rachel by twenty kilos. But it didn't matter. Rachel had her on her back, on the table, scattering dishes and food everywhere. Rachel leaned over Jessica and in a voice of cold steel, said, "Don't. Touch. Me."

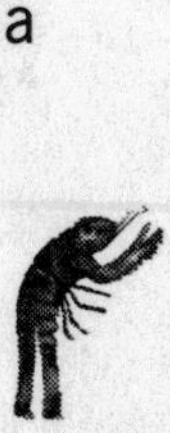

I saw Jake across the room. Too far away to intervene. Cassie was with him. It was up to me.

I jumped up and raced to Rachel. I took a deep breath and shoved both my arms between them.

"Back off, Marco," Rachel said.

"Get her off me! She's crazy!" Jessica cried.

I pushed against Rachel, trying to force her off Jessica. Suddenly, Jessica started lashing out. I assume she was trying to hit Rachel.

She missed.

"Ow!" I grabbed my left eye. "What are you hitting *me* for?"

And that's when the first teacher showed up.

Five minutes later, Jessica, Rachel and I were sitting in the assistant principal's office.

Chapman's office.

Jessica was acting outraged in a very loud voice. Rachel was staring stonily ahead. I was wondering whether my eye would just keep swelling up.

Chapman glared at us. "What is the meaning of this?" he demanded. "Fighting in the dining-hall? And you, Rachel, of all people!"

"What, like you think she's better than me?" Jessica demanded.

Chapman ignored her. He focused on Rachel. "Is something the matter? Mr Halloram says *you* started the fight. Are you OK, Rachel? Is there some kind of stress in your life?"

For a split second, I was afraid. The look in Rachel's eyes was dangerous. I had this terrible flash of her saying, "Yeah, Mr Chapman, I am a little stressed. I nearly got killed turning into an ant to sneak into your basement to fight you and the rest of your evil Yeerk friends."

I knew Rachel was too cool for anything like that. But then, I would have said she was too cool to start a fight in the dining-hall.

"It's my fault, Mr Chapman," I said.

"*Your* fault?" His eyes narrowed.

"Yes, sir. Um, they were fighting over me. See, they both want me. They're both madly in love with me, and I can certainly understand why. Can't you?"

"Are you crazy, you little toad?!" Jessica shrieked.

But when I glanced over at Rachel I saw just the slightest little tugging at the corner of her mouth. The beginnings of a smile.

Chapman yelled at us for a few minutes and told us all to make appointments with the school counseller. Then he let us go.

In the hallway outside his office, Rachel walked with me.

"I wish I could do that," she said.

"What?"

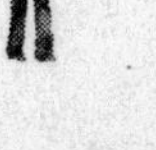

"Always think things are funny. It's why you're so . . . you know, cool and in control."

"Me? Cool and in control?" The idea surprised me. Rachel thought I was in control?

"Yesterday . . . last night . . . it got to me," she said. She shrugged. Then she smiled her supermodel smile at me. "You grind my nerves sometimes, Marco, always joking like you do. But keep it up, OK? We need a sense of humour."

"Humour? You thought I was kidding? You mean, you and Jessica aren't both insanely in love with me?"

"Dream on, Marco," she said.

Chapter 16

Ax finished building his distress beacon. He had it ready the next day, now that he had the Z-Space transponder.

Now we just had to figure out where to lay our trap. It couldn't be anywhere that would ever be connected with us. Not Cassie's farm, or the nearby woods. Not even anywhere in town, if we could help it.

A couple of days after the ant episode, we joined up again in the fields of Cassie's farm, up against the trees of the forest. This was one area we definitely had to keep safe. It was the only place we had to keep Ax if this mission to help him escape failed.

It was Tobias who came up with the answer.

<There's a gravel quarry. It's further inland. There's never anyone there. And it is just about an hour's flying time away.>

"If we're flying somewhere we'll have to get Ax a bird morph of some type," Jake said. He looked at Cassie.

"We have a few choices in the barn," she said. She bit her lip, thinking. "We have a northern harrier that was poisoned. About your size, Tobias."

"Ax? Do you mind picking up a bird morph?" Jake asked.

<I have admired Tobias's shape. It is truly wonderful in every way. The sharp talons. The beak. Much better than the human body. Not that I mean to offend. It is just that humans have no natural weapons. I miss my tail when I am in human morph.>

"No offence taken," I said. "But you're wrong about humans having no natural weapons. You marinate human feet in a pair of old training shoes for a few hours on a hot day and you'll see a deadly weapon. The dreaded stink-foot."

"OK. That's settled," Jake said. "Now, let's get down to details. If we're going to call down a Bug fighter we need to have a plan ready. I think Saturday should be the day."

"As long as it doesn't involve ants," I said. I meant it as a joke. But no one laughed.

"No ants," Jake agreed quietly.

I shook my head in amusement. "You know, we're talking about taking on Hork-Bajir and Taxxons. I used to think they were the scariest things in the world. But it's the little ant that scares me worst now."

When the meeting broke up I hung around till Jake was done saying goodbye to Cassie.

Jake and I walked home together. For a while we talked about the normal kinds of things we used to talk about before. Before our lives changed.

We talked about basketball and disagreed over which was the best NBA team. We talked about music. Neither of us had bought a new CD recently. We even talked about whether Spiderman could beat up Batman or vice versa.

You know, stupid, normal, everyday stuff.

I was stalling because I didn't want to have to tell him what I had decided.

But Jake's been my friend forever. He knows me.

"Marco? What's the problem?"

"What do you mean?"

"I mean, you haven't said a single mean-yet-funny thing the whole way. That's not you."

I laughed. Then, I just blurted it out. "This is my last time," I said.

"What do you mean?"

He knew exactly what I meant, of course. "I'm in for this time, but that's it. No more after that. And I'm serious. No one is going to 'guilt' me into it. I've done enough."

He thought about that for a while as we walked. "You're right. You have done enough. You've done a million times more than 'enough'."

"It's just been too many close calls."

"Yeah."

"One of these days we aren't going to pull it off, you know? Ten more seconds and those ants would have had us. And before that it was a pot of boiling water. And before that I was practically killed by sharks. I mean, come on. Enough is enough."

"You're right," Jake said.

"Yeah."

I was surprised that he took it so well. I guess I shouldn't have been. We all kind of treat Jake like he's the leader, but he's never been pushy about it.

"What are you going to do on Sunday?" he asked.

That took me by surprise again. "I don't know. Some Sundays we go to my mum's grave. Leave flowers and all. But this is the two-year thing." I shrugged. "I don't know, man."

He just nodded.

"But I'll tell you one thing, Jake. A year from now I don't want my dad going to leave flowers at *two* graves."

Chapter 14

<This is wonderful! Wonderful! Flying!>

The six of us were all together. Flying. It was the first time for Ax. He just kept saying how wonderful it was. He wouldn't shut up. It was the most excited he'd been since he'd discovered coffee.

Which was cool, because flying really *is* wonderful.

<These are excellent eyes!> Ax said. <Far better than your human eyes. Even better than my Andalite eyes.>

<Yes, birds of prey usually have great day-time vision,> Tobias said. <I think mine may actually be a little better than yours, though.>

<I doubt that,> Ax said. <It is hard to

imagine better vision than this.>

<Remember the good old days?> I asked. <When we used to argue over who had the best jump shot? Now it's who has the best bird eyes.>

We were sailing above a patch of woods. It was almost solid green below us. We had risen high on a beautiful thermal. A thermal is a warm bubble of air that acts like a lift, letting you soar high with almost no effort.

We hoped there were no bird-watchers down in the woods. We made a very unlikely flock — a red-tailed hawk, a falcon, a harrier, a bald eagle, and two ospreys. We kept some distance between us so it wouldn't be too obvious that we were all together.

Also, the eagle, who was Rachel, was carrying something that looked like a small TV remote control. She was the biggest bird. She got stuck lifting the weight.

<I have an idea,> I said. <Let's just blow off this suicide mission and spend the day flying around.>

<Sounds good to me,> Cassie said. She meant it to be lighthearted. It sounded just a little too serious.

<There's the quarry,> Tobias announced. <Dead ahead.>

<Dead ahead. Excellent choice of words,> I said.

We made a large circle over the area, looking for anyone who might be in the woods. But there was no one.

We spiralled down from the sky. Down into the deep, open gash in the earth that was the gravel quarry. It was a desolate place. Just a big hole in the ground with some water in the lowest spots.

A few minutes later we were back in our usual forms. Minus shoes, of course. And wearing our motley collection of morphing clothes.

"We look like a trapeze act from a circus," I said. "Way too much Spandex."

"Don't start with the uniforms again," Rachel said.

It was an old debate. I would say how we needed some decent superhero uniforms. You know, like the X-Men or whatever.

But now, I realized, I shouldn't be talking that way. As if we were all going to be together in the future.

I couldn't tell if Jake had told the others that I was quitting. Probably he had told Cassie. I doubted Rachel knew, or she would have said something. The same with Tobias.

And Ax? Who knew with Ax? He was still a mystery to us. It was one of the things I would miss after I quit. I mean, how often do you get to hang out with a real alien?

That and the flying. I would miss the flying. But if I was out, I had to be out all the way.

I guess I must have looked morose, sitting there on a pile of rocks, thinking. Jake came over and kind of gave me a shove. You know, in a friendly way.

"Come on. We need to go back under that overhang. Out of sight."

"Great," I said. "The rocks will fall and crush us and we won't have to worry about the Yeerks."

There was a sort of shallow cave in the quarry wall. Not deep at all, but it would hide us from anyone flying over.

"Well," Jake said. "Let's try this out. Ax? You ready to trigger that thing?"

<Yes. I am very ready, Prince Jake.>

Jake looked around at everyone. "You all ready to go into your various morphs?"

We nodded. All except Ax. See, we were all going to go into morph — our strongest, deadliest morphs — in order to take care of the Yeerk crew when they came. But Ax didn't have anything but a shark, a lobster, an ant, and a harrier. We figured he was better off in his own Andalite body, which was plenty dangerous.

"OK, Ax? Do it. Everyone? Morph!"

"And let's keep our fingers crossed," I added. "Or talons, claws, or hooves, as the case may be."

Ax pressed a button on the distress beacon. As far as we could tell, nothing happened.

<It is working,> he reassured us.

So, Rachel, Cassie, Jake and I began to morph. These were all morphs that we had done before. There would be no battles to maintain our control over the animal minds.

Rachel went into her elephant morph. We figured we might need that brute strength and size.

Jake slowly became a tiger. Cassie used her wolf morph. And I focused on my gorilla.

"What a freak scene this is." I laughed as the changes began. "Anyone who stumbled on to this would think he'd lost his mind."

It was definitely odd. You haven't seen weird till you've seen pretty, blonde supermodel Rachel grow a trunk as thick as a small tree and ears the size of umbrellas.

Or Cassie, growing short grey fur over every centimetre of her body, falling to all fours and baring long yellow teeth.

And then there was Jake. Huge, curved claws grew from his fingers. A snake-like tail whipped out behind him. Orange and black fur covered him. And when he was done he was a full grown tiger. Over three metres from his nose to his tail. Easily one hundred and eighty kilogrammes.

If something deadly can ever be beautiful,

it's a tiger.

<Bet I could kick your butt,> I said to Jake.

<Yeah, monkey boy? I don't *think* so.>

<Hey, I could stomp both of you,> Rachel said. She walked closer, swinging her trunk and flaring her ears out. A moving mountain.

<This is *so* mature,> Cassie said. <Arguing over who could beat who.>

<Hah. You're only saying that because we can all kick your butt, wolfie,> I pointed out.

<As if!> Cassie protested. <You'd have to catch me first. And I could still be running long after the three of you were worn out and fast asleep.>

<You have an amazing variety of animals on your planet,> Ax said. <Some day, when the Yeerks are defeated, Andalites will come here simply to try out the many animal forms. It would be like a holiday.>

<Joe Andalite, you've won the Superbowl! Now where are you going?> I said, mimicking the Disney World commercials. <I'm going to Earth to turn into a lobster!>

<I don't understand,> Ax said.

I started to explain, but just then a red light began to flash on Ax's homemade distress beacon. <The response signal! They are coming!>

<Quick! Everyone to your places!> Jake said.

He slunk away, liquid power, to hide in the

shadow of a boulder. Rachel pressed back under the shallow overhang. Cassie trotted to a spot to the right of Jake, and I tried not to look like a two-hundred-kilogramme gorilla behind a pile of gravel. Tobias flapped his wings hard, struggling to gain altitude.

SWOOSH!

It came in low and fast, just above tree level, then disappeared before turning to come back.

A Bug fighter. Just as we'd planned.

<Here's your ride home, Ax,> I said.

Chapter 18

Swoosh!

The Bug fighter flew over once again, seemed to pause, then settled down towards the floor of the quarry.

Bug fighters are the smallest of the Yeerk ships. They aren't much bigger than a school bus. They have a cowled, insect-like look, except that on either side there are very long, serrated spears pointing forward. So they look a little like a cockroach holding two spears.

The Bug fighter landed as gently as a feather.

I held my breath.

<Wait for it,> Jake said. <Wait for it.>

The hatch opened. Out stepped a Hork-Bajir Controller.

The Andalite prince, Ax's brother, had told us that the Hork-Bajir were a good, decent people who had been enslaved against their will by the Yeerks.

Uh-huh. Maybe so. But what they looked like was a whole different thing. Hork-Bajir are big, walking razor blades. They're about two metres tall, two arms, two legs, and a nasty spiked tail similar to Andalite tails.

There are swordlike blades raked forward from their snake heads. There are also blades at their elbows and wrists and knees.

I mean, let me put it this way: If Klingons were real, they would be scared of Hork-Bajir.

<Get ready.> Jake again.

The Hork-Bajir stepped clear of the Bug fighter. Then, he just stood there.

<There will be a Taxxon inside,> Ax reminded us.

<Yeah. We know,> I said.

Why was the Hork-Bajir just standing there? He should be looking around. After all, he was answering a distress beacon. Why was he just standing there like he was waiting for something?

<On the count of three,> Jake said in our heads. <One . . . Two . . . Three!>

"Tsseeeeerrrr!"

Tobias swooped, falling from the sky at close

to a hundred and sixty kilometres an hour. He raked his talons forward and hit the Hork-Bajir's face.

"RROOWWWRR!" Jake leaped from cover. He sailed through the air and hit the Hork-Bajir with paws outstretched, claws bared.

The Hork-Bajir went down hard.

Jake rolled away as the Hork-Bajir slashed the air like an out-of-control blender.

But just then Rachel rumbled up, as big as a tank.

<OK, back off, Jake,> Rachel said. <I have him.>

She pressed one big, tree-stump leg on the Hork-Bajir's chest and pressed him down against the ground. She did not crush him, just held him like a bug who could easily be squashed.

The Hork-Bajir decided it was time to stop struggling and lie very still.

Too easy, a part of my mind warned me. *Too easy. No Hork-Bajir Controller had ever just given up like that.*

But I had other problems. My job was to get inside the Bug fighter. Get the Taxxon pilot.

<Let's go!> I yelled.

I ran forward, loping clumsily on my gorilla legs, swinging my massive, mighty gorilla arms. Cassie and Ax were right there with me. Taxxons are disgusting, oversized centipedes, but I wasn't

worried. We were more than enough to handle a Taxxon.

But then —

Zzzzzzzzaaapppp!

A brilliant red beam of light sliced the air just inches in front of me. It blocked my way.

Zzzzzzzzaaaapppp!

Another beam of blinding red light. This crossed behind me. It exploded gravel into steam as it traced a path!

<Dracon beams!> Ax cried.

I spun around, looking for cover.

Zzzzzzaaaaappppp!

<Look!> Cassie screamed in our heads. <Up on the edge of the quarry!>

I looked, as the Dracon beams formed a cage of deadly light around us. The edge of the quarry above was lined with Hork-Bajir. I looked left. More! To the right . . . more!

The entire quarry was lined with Hork-Bajir warriors, each armed with a Dracon beam. There must have been a hundred of them. We were surrounded.

Completely surrounded.

<Stay in morph,> Jake snapped. <Don't let them know we're human.>

<Let's charge them!> Rachel yelled.

<No! You can't even climb up that rock face. Don't be stupid!>

Cassie called Tobias. <Tobias! You can get away!>

<I don't think so,> he said. <No headwind. It would take me a couple of minutes to flap my way up out of here. They'd fry me before I got clear.>

The reality settled over us. The despair.

<What are we going to do?> Cassie wailed.

<There has to be a way out! There *has* to be!> Rachel yelled.

<Not this time,> I said grimly.

We were trapped. Outnumbered. Outsmarted. Finished.

And that was when *he* came.

Chapter 19

He looked so much like Ax. So much like Prince Elfangor. And yet, somehow, totally different. The difference wasn't something you saw. This was something you felt.

A shadow on your soul. The darkness that blotted out the light of the sun. Evil. Destruction.

Not the impersonal, programmed destructiveness of the ants. This was warm-blooded, deliberate evil.

His body was an Andalite. He was the only Andalite-Controller in existence. The only Yeerk ever to infest an Andalite body. The only Yeerk with the Andalite power to morph.

Visser Three.

Visser Three, who had murdered the Andalite Prince Elfangor while we cowered in terror.

Visser Three, who even the Hork-Bajir and Taxxons feared.

<Well, well,> he said, thought-speaking to us. <I have you at last, my brave Andalite bandits. Fools. Do you think we never change our frequencies?>

<*Yeerk!*> Ax said in a silent voice loaded with hatred.

Visser Three's main eyes focused on Ax. <A little one,> he said, surprised. <Are the Andalites now reduced to using their children to fight?>

Ax started to say something, but Jake snapped, <Shut up, Ax! None of us communicates with *him*. Give him nothing.>

Ax fell silent, but he was practically vibrating with rage and hatred for the Yeerk Visser. It wasn't surprising. Visser Three had killed his brother.

But Jake was right. We couldn't get into a conversation with Visser Three. The rest of us wanted to hide the fact that we were humans, not Andalites. We could too easily slip and reveal the truth.

Visser Three seemed to be enjoying his big moment. <What a colourful assortment of morphs,> he said. <Earth has such wonderful

animals, don't you agree? When we have enslaved the humans and made this planet over in *our* image, we will have to be sure and keep some of these forms alive. It would be entertaining to try some of these morphs myself.>

None of us said anything. At least not anything that was human. Jake did snarl, drawing his tiger lip back over his teeth.

<Especially you,> Visser Three said to Jake. <That is a beautiful, deadly animal. I approve. In fact, I was going to demand you demorph. But I have a better idea. You see, we have a guest aboard the mother ship. It will be entertaining to show you to Visser One as you are.>

I was sick with dread and fear. But not so afraid that I didn't notice a sneer in Visser Three's tone when he said "Visser One."

<Did you catch that?> Jake asked me in the thought-speak version of a whisper.

<Yeah. Visser Three doesn't like Visser One.>

Visser Three must have given some signal, because at that moment his Blade ship appeared overhead, shimmering into view as it decloaked.

The Blade ship is far larger than the Bug fighters, and very different. It is jet-black. It's built like some kind of battle-axe from the middle ages, with two curved axe-head wings, and a long, diamond-pointed "handle" aimed forward.

<We're better off making a run for it!> Rachel said.

<It would be suicide,> I said. <As long as we're alive, there's hope.>

<Yeah. Visser Three is taking us to the Yeerk mother ship to show off for his boss. Some hope.>

But Rachel did nothing. And I did nothing. And we all just stood there, under the watchful eyes of a hundred Hork-Bajir.

They must have landed out of sight while we were busy watching the one Bug fighter.

Ax had used the wrong frequency. The Yeerks had figured out we were laying a trap. And our trap had become Visser Three's trap.

A couple of dozen Hork-Bajir leaped down from the high wall of the quarry and surrounded us. They kept their Dracon beams levelled at us as the Blade ship landed on the quarry floor.

"Go, obey *farghurrash* there *horlit*!" one of the Hork-Bajir said, in the strange mix of English and their own language that they use.

He pointed to the Blade ship. A door had opened in the side.

<I can't fit in there,> Rachel said.

But as she approached the door, the door widened to her size. It stretched and grew as if the metal skin of the Blade ship were alive.

What a pathetic little crew we were, trooping

inside the Blade ship. Weak and pathetic and stupid to imagine that we could ever have stopped the Yeerks.

Visser Three was right. We were fools.

This wasn't even my fight, I thought. Not really. This wasn't my time to die.

I guess I wanted to feel angry. But what I felt was numb, as I trooped into the Blade ship with the others. You know, like I wasn't really there, almost. I was past feeling anything, I guess. I just kept thinking, *It's happening. It's finally really happening.*

The next day was Sunday. My dad would go to my mum's grave. Alone.

It would be a while before he would admit that I, too, was gone.

Just like when my mum died — there would never be a body.

Just like my mum.

Chapter 20

<This is not looking good,> I said. I couldn't take the silence any more.

<No. It isn't. But we're not dead yet,> Jake answered.

<Yet. Why doesn't that make me happy?> I asked. I looked around at the others, all crammed into a windowless steel cube. Black, dimly lit steel walls on all six sides. No door. It was like a coffin.

<We look like some kind of circus,> I said. <An elephant, a tiger, a gorilla, a wolf, and a freak of nature.>

That got some halfhearted laughs from the others. I don't know why I was making jokes. I guess that's the way I am. Whenever bad things

happen, I tell jokes. But inside I felt sick. Like I had swallowed broken glass.

<Maybe we should just demorph,> Cassie said. <Maybe if they realize we aren't Andalites, they'll let us go.>

She knew that was dumb, of course. But when you're scared, you start grabbing at anything. You want to believe there's a way out.

The truth was, there were exactly two possibilities. Visser Three would kill us. Or Visser Three would turn us into Controllers. He would infest us with a Yeerk.

<We should stay in animal morph,> Jake said. <I mean, the thing is, if Visser Three learns we are human, he may go after our families next. He may figure we told them something.>

<Prince Jake is right,> Ax said. <The Yeerks will not want to take the chance of other humans knowing of them.>

It was true. I knew it was true. I guess I'd known it all along. But hearing it said, it made me want to crawl into a corner.

My dad. Cassie's parents. Rachel's mum and her sisters. Jake's parents. Maybe even Jake's brother, Tom, although he was one of *them.* Their lives were at risk, too.

Suddenly, a window opened in one of the walls. It just grew, the same way the door had done before. Like the steel was alive. It formed a round porthole, large enough for all of us to see — even Rachel, who could only turn her massive head enough to look with one eye.

I gasped.

Below us, blue and white and so beautiful it brought tears to your eyes, was Earth.

Sun sparkled off the ocean. Clouds swirled over the Gulf of Mexico, a big spiral, maybe a hurricane.

<Look,> Cassie said simply.

We looked. Through the eyes of the animals of Earth, but with the minds of human beings, we looked down at our planet.

Our planet.

For now, at least. For a little while longer.

Then something different came into view, as the Blade ship rotated away from Earth.

<This is why the Yeerks opened a window,> Ax said. <This is what they wanted us to see. So that we would despair.>

The mother ship.

It was a gigantic, three-legged insect. The centre was a single, bloated sphere. The sphere was flatter on the bottom, and from the bottom hung a weird, mismatched series of tendrils. Like the tendrils of a jellyfish. Each one must have been a kilometre long.

Around the sphere were three legs, bent up, then back down, exactly like a spider's legs.

<The legs are the engines,> Ax explained. <The tendrils hanging down below the belly are weapons and sensors and energy collectors. That is also where the shipboard Kandrona is. The Yeerks must bathe in the Yeerk pool every three days and absorb Kandrona rays. There must be one on the planet below, too.>

<Yeah. We know,> I said. <Your brother told us. For all the good it did us.>

It just hung in orbit, like a predator gazing down hungrily at blue Earth below.

<I can't believe people on Earth don't see this on radar,> Rachel said. <I mean, it's huge. It's a city!>

<It is shielded,> Ax said simply. <It cannot be seen by radar. And it would normally be invisible to us. Visser Three is showing it to us. To terrify us.>

<He's doing a good job,> I said.

<I've never been in space before,> Cassie said. <I always wished I could. I always wanted to see Earth, all in one piece like that.>

<It is a lovely planet,> Ax said gently. <Not so different from mine. Except that we have less ocean and more grassland. I . . . I am sorry I brought you all to this. This is my fault.>

I wanted to yell, "Yes! Yes, it is your fault!"

But Cassie said what we all knew in our hearts. <Ax, you only came here because your

people wanted to protect us. Your brother and a lot of Andalites died trying to save us. Nothing is your fault.>

It was true. But sometimes, when everything hits the fan, you don't want the truth. You just want someone to blame. <One too many missions,> I muttered. <This was going to be my last one. Now . . . well, it will still be my last one.>

I could see an opening in the side of the Yeerk mother ship — a docking port. As I watched, a pair of quick Bug fighters flew in, dwarfed by the size of the opening.

A minute later, we entered the docking port and were suddenly bathed in deep red light.

Through the window, we could see Yeerk crewmen — Hork-Bajir, Taxxons, and two or three other alien species, in simple red or dark brown uniforms. And there were humans, too. My first reaction was hope. Humans!

But then I realized the truth. No. Human-Controllers. Yeerks. No different from the Hork-Bajir.

There was a slight shudder as the Blade ship came to a halt.

<Ax?> Jake asked. <What's our morph time?>

<We have been in morph for forty per cent of allowable time.>

I did the maths. <So we've had forty-eight minutes. Leaving what, seventy-two minutes?>

<Yeah,> Tobias confirmed. <Not a lot of time for you guys. Maybe Rachel is right. Maybe we should just go out in a blaze of glory. Attack as soon as they open the door. At least we can let them know we were here.>

I saw Jake extend his claws, as if he were thinking about using them. He glanced at where the door had once been, like he was measuring the distance. I knew that he was listening to the tiger in his head.

Then he seemed to relax. <No,> he said. <We have to have hope.>

Cassie sidled up next to him and nuzzled him with her wolf's muzzle.

I guess it should have been funny. The wolf and the tiger, sharing a tender moment. But all it did was make me a little jealous. They had each other.

<We gave them a pretty good fight, didn't we?> I said. <Our little circus? We did some damage to them.>

<Yes, we did,> Rachel agreed.

<Do . . .> Ax hesitated. Then, <Do humans fear death?>

<Yes. We're not crazy about death,> I answered. <How about Andalites?>

<We're also not crazy about it.>

Through the window we could see a lot of Hork-Bajir and Taxxons and humans running around, racing to get somewhere. They were all lining up. And now, I noticed, there were distinct kinds of uniforms, one red-and-black, the other gold-and-black. The brown uniforms were all around the edges, like they were less important.

Suddenly, without warning, the window stretched open into a large, arched doorway. Foetid air rushed in, smelling of oil and chemicals and something else.

A ramp rose up from the steel floor outside to meet us. We were standing like a display at the top of the ramp. All around, filling this side of the docking bay, were uniformed Hork-Bajir, Taxxons, and humans. Most were in red-and-black. Perhaps two hundred creatures, standing in stiff rows, arranged by species.

About a quarter of the total were in gold-and-black. There were more humans in this group, but also some unusually massive Hork-Bajir.

<Jake? I have a feeling. I don't think the reds like the golds.>

<I think they belong to two different Vissers,> Ax said. <I . . . I think I overheard my brother talk about that. Each Visser has his own private army in their own uniforms.>

<Swell. I wonder which group gets to have us?> I said.

Far at the back of the rows of alien troops, there was a movement. A party of creatures

walking to the front.

Visser Three was at the centre, followed by two big Hork-Bajir in red.

And just to his left was a human. A human woman with dark hair and very dark eyes.

That was when I stopped breathing. Because I knew. Even before I could see her face clearly. I knew.

They marched up to the bottom of the ramp. A dozen soldiers levelled Dracon beams at us, just in case we wanted any trouble.

Then, in thought-speak that all could hear, Visser Three turned to the woman beside him. <You see, Visser One. I have taken the Andalite bandits. The crisis is over. Your trip here is wasted, and you can return to the home world.>

Visser One nodded. She looked up at us with those dark brown, human eyes.

Eyes I knew. Eyes I remembered.

The same eyes that watched me sleep every night from the framed picture beside my bed.

My mother.

Visser One.

Chapter 21

I sat down. Very suddenly. I'm sure it looked funny. A big, hairy gorilla simply falling down.

I would have laughed if I'd seen it.

My mother. Not dead.

Alive!

I wanted to yell. "Mum! Mum! It's me, Marco!"

But Jake's voice was in my head, a loud, urgent whisper. <Marco? Don't say anything. Don't do anything. Do you hear me?>

So I wasn't just imagining it. Jake had recognized her, too.

<Marco? Listen to me, man. You have to hold it together.>

My mother . . . alive.

My mum.

<Come on, Marco, stand up. Don't make them suspicious.> He was speaking just to me.

I could hear Jake. I could. But it seemed to come from far off. He didn't understand. It was my *mum.* My mum!

<Marco? That is not your mother. Not any more. That is *not* her.>

<Jake? It's my mum. Look, it's her.>

<No, it isn't, Marco. Not any more. They have her. She's one of them. One of *them*!>

<Why, Visser One,> Visser Three sneered, <you seem to have frightened the humanoid one.>

"It is called a gorilla," Visser One said coldly. "If you are going to be in charge of Earth, Visser Three, you should at least learn something about the planet."

<And take a human host body, like you did? No, I think not. Human bodies are weak. I much prefer this Andalite host.>

My mother looked at him and curled her lip. "I took a human host and learned about the planet and the humans. And because of that I was able to begin the invasion that you have now endangered with your criminal incompetence!"

Visser Three's deadly Andalite tail twitched, as if he was going to stab my mum . . . Visser One. The red troops tensed up. The gold troops let their hands edge towards their weapons.

<OK,> Rachel said. <I think we were right. These two definitely don't like each other.>

She didn't know, I realized slowly. Rachel didn't know. But she had never met my mother. Neither had Cassie or Tobias. And Jake had kept our talk private.

Visser Three slowly relaxed. <You would *like* to provoke me, Visser One,> he said. <But the fact is that I destroyed the Andalite force. I shot down their dome ship. I killed Prince Elfangor myself and heard his dying screams. And now I have eliminated this last, tiny, pathetic rabble of Andalites.>

My mum . . . Visser One . . . just smiled. "You want to be Visser One? You think you can take my title? We shall see. The Council of Thirteen does not like Vissers who make mistakes. And you have made many mistakes. Be careful of your own ambition."

She snapped her fingers, and every one of the soldiers in gold turned. Then she walked away, followed by her gold-uniformed troops.

That was not my mother. At least not the creature who called herself Visser One.

Visser One was the Yeerk inside my mother's brain.

But the sickening thing is, you see, that the host mind is still alive, still aware. Somewhere inside that head, behind those painfully familiar eyes, my mother still lived.

<Take it easy, Marco,> Jake said. <I know how it is. I know how much you want to do something. But now is not the time. They'd cut us down before we got two steps.>

<I know,> I said dully. I hated myself for not trying, but I knew there was nothing I could do. I had to hide inside my morph. Never let my mother know it was me. Never let her know . . .

Slowly, heavily, I stood up. I felt weak. A very strange feeling for a gorilla.

I think right then, if I had been in any other morph I would have just surrendered and let the animal mind take over. Let instinct rule, and wash away my human emotion.

But the gorilla was too much like a human. Its instincts were gentle. Like humans, it was a creature with emotions. It could not protect me from the pain.

<Don't tell the others, Jake,> I said. <You're the only one who recognized her.>

<OK, Marco.>

<You can't even tell Cassie, OK?>

<It's OK, man. You are my oldest and best friend. You know that. No one will ever know from me.>

Visser Three still stared at us. I think he wasn't sure what to do next.

<Six Andalites,> he said. <Six Andalite

bodies that could be used by my loyal lieutenants.>

Ax exploded. <And then there would be others like you, you filth! Other Andalite-Controllers. More unnatural abominations like your vile self!>

Visser Three cocked his head thoughtfully. <Why are you the only one who speaks? You're right of course: Why would I allow anyone else to acquire Andalite morphing powers? But you are a child. Why do the others remain silent? And why do you all still hide in your morphs? Curious. Very curious.>

He seemed to think it over for a minute. Would he realize the truth? Would he figure out that the reason we remained silent was so he wouldn't guess that we were human? Would he figure out that's why we stayed in morph?

He seemed to shrug.

<Take them back to a holding cell. Triple the guard. If there is the slightest trouble, kill them all.>

Chapter 22

They marched us down a hallway. Rachel, still in her huge elephant body, filled the hallway like our ant bodies had filled the tunnels in the sand. Tobias rode on my shoulder, unable to fly in the cramped space.

The place we ended up was just like the bare, black-steel prison we'd been held in on the Blade ship. But this time no window appeared.

There was dim light that seemed to radiate from the ceiling. But nothing else at all.

I slumped down in a corner.

<What's our time look like, Ax?> Jake asked.

<You have only thirty per cent of your time left.>

<Thirty-six minutes,> Jake translated.

<Thirty-six minutes and I'll spend the rest of my life as an elephant,> Rachel said. <Not that the 'rest of my life' is likely to be much time.>

For a while everyone talked about various plans for escape. It was all just talk. We knew we were trapped. We knew it was over. We were aboard the Yeerk mother ship. It was huge. If we had a week to learn our way around, we'd still have been lost in its maze.

There were hundreds, probably thousands of armed Yeerks — Hork-Bajir, Taxxons, and a few other shapes we'd never seen before, and of course, humans.

Like my mother.

My mother — Visser One. Most powerful of the Vissers.

When had it happened? Had the Yeerks taken her much earlier? Had she already been a Controller for those last years when she was with us?

When she had come to my bedroom to say good night, had that been a Yeerk slug, just playing a part, like an actor?

When I tried to fake sick to get out of school, had it been a Yeerk who saw through my story and kidded and joked me into admitting it?

Was it a Yeerk, handing out the presents on Christmas morning? A Yeerk, singing in the church choir? A Yeerk, pulling the puppet strings of my mother's body when she dragged me through J. C. Penney's and made me buy school clothes I didn't really like?

Was it a Yeerk I used to find making out with my dad like a teenager when they didn't think I saw them?

All of it an act? All of it fake? For how many years?

How much of what I'd thought was my mother, had been . . . one of *them*?

One thing was sure. Her death had been faked. The so-called drowning accident. No body recovered.

But the body *had* been recovered, hadn't it? The Yeerks' mission had been accomplished. The invasion of Earth had been started. Visser One was leaving Earth in the hands of Visser Three. And so she had to disappear and not leave anyone asking questions.

<There has to be *something* we can do!> Rachel was saying.

Ax said, <My people have a saying — grace is the acceptance of the inevitable.>

<Yeah?> I said suddenly. <Well, actually I don't *accept.* That's what *they* want. They want the entire human race to lie down and accept the inevitable.>

Jake turned his big, yellow tiger eyes on me. I saw Tobias's eternally fierce glare.

I stood up.

<I have a saying for you. I got it from a fortune cookie. 'Fall down seven times, get up eight.' You know what that means? That means you don't ever just lie there. You always get up. You always come back for more. You never surrender. Maybe you die, but you never surrender.>

They were all looking at me now. Through the eyes of a wolf and a hawk and the big, sad eyes of an elephant.

<Ants,> I said. <We can morph to ants again.>

Cassie was shocked. <You're saying that? You? I thought you hated those ant morphs as much as I did.>

<I did. But it may work. We morph to ants. Maybe there's a crack here somewhere. We try and escape into the walls and the machines. We can hide, then morph into something more dangerous, attack, and then disappear again. Maybe even find a way to destroy the Kandrona.>

<That's nuts,> Rachel said. <I like it.>

<At least we can hurt them before they catch up with us,> Jake agreed cautiously. <Except for Tobias.>

<You have to do what's right for the group,> Tobias said. <I'll have to take my chances. I'd feel better knowing you guys were still out there somewhere, making trouble for the Yeerks.>

<It may work,> Ax said. <The Yeerks are not

very familiar with morphing, except for Visser Three. They may not expect an insect morph.>

<All right, then,> Jake said. <Let's —>

The door opened. It simply appeared silently in the wall.

Standing there were three Hork-Bajir. They were wearing gold uniforms.

Lying on the floor were four other Hork-Bajir. They were each uniformed in red. Lying either dead or unconscious.

<Don't move,> Jake snapped as he saw Rachel and me tensing up for a charge.

The lead Hork-Bajir, a huge creature maybe two and a half metres tall with head blades that were more than a metre long, eyed us.

He spoke. It was surprising, because he did not speak the usual strange mishmash of languages the Hork-Bajir used. This one sounded like he'd been educated at Harvard.

"This hallway goes on in that direction for thirty metres." He pointed to his left. "Then comes a guard station, where there will be two Hork-Bajir and a Taxxon. From there, four hallways. Take the one furthest to your left. Follow it to a central dropshaft. Take the dropshaft down fifteen decks. Directly ahead you will see escape pods."

He looked at Rachel. "You are too large in that morph to fit in the escape pod. You will need to demorph when you get there. The pod is programmed to return you to the planet in the same area where you were seized. The pod will then self-destruct. Do you understand?"

We all just stared.

<It's a trap,> Tobias said.

<No. We're already trapped. They could kill us any time,> I said.

<Marco's right,> Jake said. <Why let us escape if they want to kill us?>

<This is one of Visser One's soldiers,> Ax pointed out. <It would be very embarrassing for Visser Three if his prisoners should escape, no?>

<Politics,> Cassie said, with a laugh. <It's about politics! Visser One is making Visser Three look bad. If we escape, it will be blamed on Visser Three.>

"You will have to deal with any of Visser Three's troops you encounter between here and the escape pod," the gold-clad Hork-Bajir said. "Leave. Now."

<Ax?> Jake asked.

<Only fifteen per cent of your morph time is left.>

<That's about eighteen minutes. Let's do it!>

Visser One's troops turned and marched away.

<I'll go in front,> Rachel said.

<OK. And let's move,> Jake said.

Rachel squeezed her massive tonnage into the hallway. <All right. Now let's see who wants to try and stop me!>

Chapter 23

Whomp! Whomp! Whomp! Whomp!

Rachel made the steel floor vibrate with each massive step. Her leathery sides scraped the corridor walls so that I could only catch occasional glimpses past her.

The hallway was empty until we reached the guard station. Just as the Hork-Bajir had said.

Rachel didn't even slow down.

Whomp! Whomp! Whomp! Whomp!

I saw a flash of a Taxxon, foolishly running as if to cut her off. A few seconds later I had to jump over the crushed remnants of the big centipede.

<Look out! Hork-Bajir!> Cassie yelled.

He exploded out of a side corridor, a red-uniformed Hork-Bajir.

Swoooosh!

A razor-bladed arm sliced the air just in front of my face.

<More coming!> Tobias warned. <Both directions! All of them in red!>

<I can't turn around!> Rachel moaned. She was too big, too tight a fit in the corridors to turn and help, as half a dozen Hork-Bajir in Visser Three's livery came screaming on to the scene.

<I knew it couldn't be that easy,> I said.

<Battle!> Ax said, sounding almost like he was announcing a party.

I felt the same way. I was ready. I was mad and tired of feeling helpless.

The closest Hork-Bajir swung at me again and sliced a ten-centimetre long cut in the matted fur of my huge shoulders.

That was all it took. Like I said, gorillas are peaceful, almost gentle creatures.

But don't go making one angry. Especially not when a boy who wants very badly to hurt some Yeerks is sharing space in the gorilla's head.

"Hoohoo hoo hhawwwwrr!" I cried and swung a fist the size of a brick into the stomach of the Hork-Bajir. I gave it all I had. I put every fibre of the gorilla's muscle into the blow.

The Hork-Bajir was lifted clear up off the deck. His head slammed the ceiling. He was down and out of the game.

Out of the corner of my eye I saw another Hork-Bajir leap at Ax. The Andalite's tail flashed forward so fast you didn't even see it move. The Hork-Bajir staggered back, minus an arm.

<Good one, Ax!>

<You as well! Hah hah!>

I decided right then — I kind of liked Ax.

<Rachel!> Jake yelled. <Keep moving. Left tunnel. Look for a dropshaft, whatever that is. The longer we stay here, the more of these guys are going to show up.>

Just then, right on cue, two more Hork-Bajir came up from behind us. <You guys move! I'll deal with them,> Jake said.

The Hork-Bajir rushed us.

"RRRRRRROOOOOWWWRRR!"

Jake let loose with a roar that must have been heard from one end of the mother ship to the other. It even scared me. And it sure made the Hork-Bajir hesitate.

He was on them, while they were still thinking about what to do next.

Hork-Bajir are very fast. But so are tigers.

One Hork-Bajir was down, with Jake sinking fangs into his snake-like neck. The other Hork-Bajir looked around to make sure no one could see him, then decided he'd like to live. He kept his distance.

Jake backed away but kept his face turned to

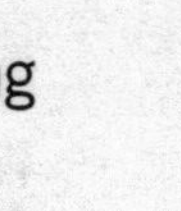

the Hork-Bajir behind us. We trotted as fast as we could down the hallway, leaving a scene of devastation.

It was like the ant tunnels. We could only try to escape. The longer we tried to fight, the more the odds would turn against us.

Suddenly . . .

<Ahhhhhhh!>

<Rachel!> I heard Tobias cry.

<It's OK. I found the dropshaft. I am . . . dropping.>

<What is it?> I asked.

<A lift without a floor,> Rachel answered.

Then I was there, at the edge of a long shaft that went down and down, maybe forever. Rachel already looked small. Which was not easy for her to do.

<He said to stop after fifteen levels!> I reminded her.

<Yeah? And how do I do that?>

<Think the number! It hears speech and understands simple thought-speak commands,> Ax instructed. Then added, <At least that's how it works on *our* ships.>

<I'm slowing down. Cool!>

<More Hork-Bajir back here! And some of those other ones. The little wrinkled ones!> Cassie yelled. <They're coming fast!>

<Here goes nothing,> I said. I took a look

down the dropshaft and jumped off into empty space.

You know, if it hadn't been for the fact that I was just a few minutes from being trapped forever in a morph, and if there weren't a dozen or so walking Salad Shooters after me, it would have been fun.

I fell, but not too fast.

<Fifteen levels,> I thought as floors zipped past me.

Twelve levels down, I plummeted past a human Controller who was getting ready to step into the dropshaft. He had a very human look of total amazement on his face. Possibly because while standing there, he'd seen a flying elephant, followed by a gorilla, a wolf, an Andalite, and a tiger.

<Hork-Bajir, coming fast!> Tobias warned.

I looked up the shaft. A big Hork-Bajir warrior was gaining on us. But there was nothing I could do until he reached us.

<He's mine,> Tobias said. He flared his wings, flapped hard and was shooting back up the dropshaft towards the falling Hork-Bajir.

"Tseeeeer!"

Tobias's talons came forward, outstretched, and slashed the alien's eyes.

"Ghaahharrr!"

The Hork-Bajir clutched at his face. I guess

he was too distracted to think about what floor he was heading to. He shot past us as we slowed to step on to the fifteenth level.

Hard floor under my feet again! A very good feeling.

<Rachel! You have to demorph!> I reminded her.

<Already working on it,> she said.

She was shrinking even as she lumbered along.

<The escape pods! Ahead there!> Ax cried.

They were only a dozen feet from us. A few seconds more and we would make it.

Rachel stumbled. She was half-human, half-elephant. A nightmare of pink and grey, with huge ears and human hair and fat arms and legs that had no feet.

I reached down and swept her up with my powerful arms. She was still large, maybe a hundred and thirty kilogrammes. But not too much for me to carry.

We reached the door of the escape pod.

It closed behind us as we wedged our over-sized bodies inside.

<Ax! Time!> Jake yelled.

<Five per cent of the time remains!>

<Six minutes. Morph out!>

There was a surge as the escape pod ejected from the underside of the Yeerk ship.

My dense black fur was already starting to disappear by the time the pod rotated. I could see Earth below.

Earth.

And as the tiny ship turned, I could see the Yeerk mother ship.

It was kind of a joke now, I thought. The Yeerk mother ship. My mother on the Yeerk mother ship.

Hah hah.

Before I became fully human again, before I lost the ability to thought-speak and had to return to words spoken out loud, I said, <Jake?>

<Yeah, Marco.>

<No one ever finds out. No one can ever know.>

<OK, Marco,> he said.

<My mother died two years ago tomorrow.>

<That's how it will be, my friend.>

<Yeah. But someday . . .> Someday, somehow, in some way that I could not foresee, we would win this battle. Humans and Andalites together would defeat the Yeerks. And we would free all of their slaves.

All of them.

<Someday,> I whispered again.

<Someday, Marco,> Jake said.

Chapter 24

I guess there's no such thing as a nice graveyard. But the place where my mum is remembered is as nice as it can be.

The grass is green. There's a tree nearby. It's always very quiet. You can smell flowers.

I hate going there.

My dad stood for a long time, looking down at the white marble headstone. It has my mum's name. The day she was born, the day she died. And a message that says, "No wife, no mother, was ever more loved. Or more deeply missed."

My dad and I stood a few feet apart. We didn't say anything. We both just kind of cried.

You probably wouldn't think I was the kind of guy who would cry. Mostly I don't. Mostly I make jokes about things. It's better to laugh than to cry, don't you think?

I do.

Even when the whole world is scary and sad. Especially when the world is scary and sad. That's when you need to laugh.

"Two years," my dad said. It surprised me.

"Yeah," I said. "Two years."

He took a deep breath. Like it was hard for him to breathe. "I . . . I . . . look, Marco, I've been thinking."

"Yes?"

"I haven't been a very good father to you." It wasn't a question, so I didn't say anything.

"Your mum . . ." He had to stop for a moment to get his voice under control. "Your mum would not be happy about the way I've been these last two years."

What could I say? I decided to say nothing.

"Anyway. I talked to Jerry the other day."

Jerry was his old boss. Back when he had a regular job.

My dad shrugged. "I guess we have to live, huh? I mean, we can't . . . you know." Another heavy breath. "Your mum wouldn't want us to give up, would she? Anyway, I'm going in Monday to talk to Jerry about getting back to work. You know . . . see if I still remember how to even turn on a computer."

It was a big thing. A big decision. I guess what I should have done was run over to give him a hug and tell him I was proud of him. I *was* proud of him. But that's not me.

"Oh, Dad, you never could figure computers out. Especially games."

He stared at me with the blank eyes I had seen for the last two years. Then, suddenly, he laughed.

"You punk kid, I've forgotten more about computers than you ever knew."

"Oh, right! So why did I always kick your butt whenever we played Doom?"

"I *let* you win."

I made an extremely rude noise. "Yeah? How about if we just go home and play a game so I can show you how totally wrong you are?"

I couldn't stop him from giving me a hug. I guess I didn't mind all that much.

We walked away from my mother's gravestone. The stone that marked the death of a woman who was not dead.

I raised my eyes up to the sky. The blue sky of Earth. My home.

She was probably gone from the mother ship, now. Off to some other corner of the galaxy.

But wherever she was, no matter how far, I would find her.

Someday . . .

Don't miss . . .

ANIMORPHS

ANIMORPHS 6:

The Capture

by K.A. Applegate

I was bounced and slammed against walls and even dropped at one point. I felt us go down a set of stairs. I felt hands grabbing at me and slipping away.

Finally, fresh air. We were running like mad for the shelter of a stand of trees that fronted the hospital.

"My . . . head . . ." I said.

<Headache? No surprise, dude.>

"Something . . . wrong . . .I can't . . . think."

<Don't worry. Take a break. We have it under control. More or less.>

<Unbelievable,> said a voice in my head. <Can it be? *Humans?*>

What was that voice? Where was it coming from?

Marco lifted me and slung me over a horse's back. Cassie.

<Cassie? A human, yes. And Rachel? The cousin? Human as well?>

. . . What was happening? There was a voice inside my head.

We were running now, running and running at full gallop, through trees, across lawns, down suburban streets where Cassie's hooves clattered loudly.

We jumped a fence. I flew through the air and landed hard on the dirt.

I felt pain, but it came from far away.

. . . I looked around. Trees, everywhere. A panting horse standing nearby.

I saw all this, but in a distant way, as if I were watching it all on TV. My eyes moved left, right. They moved all on their own. Like someone else was focusing them.

Cassie. I tried to say her name. Cassie.

But no sound came from my mouth.

<Don't struggle, Jake,> a voice in my head said. <It's pointless.>

What? Who was saying that? What was . . . ?

Then, a laugh that only I could hear. <Put

that primitive human brain to work, Jake. Jake the Animorph,> it sneered. <Jake, the servant of the Andalite filth!>

Then I knew.

I knew what the voice was.

A Yeerk!

A Yeerk in my own head.

I was a Controller. . .

Brand New Ancients

KATE TEMPEST was born in 1985 and grew up in South-East London, where she still lives. She started out as a rapper, toured the spoken word circuit for a number of years and began writing for theatre in 2012. Her work includes the album *Balance*, recorded with Sound of Rum; *Everything Speaks in its Own Way*, a collection of poems published on her own imprint Zingaro; *GlassHouse*, a forum theatre play for Cardboard Citizens; and the plays *Wasted* and *Hopelessly Devoted* for Paines Plough, both published by Methuen. Her epic narrative poem *Brand New Ancients* won the Ted Hughes Prize in 2013 and is published by Picador; it completed a sell-out run in the UK and New York and won a Herald Angel at Edinburgh Fringe. *Everybody Down*, her debut solo album, was released on Big Dada Records in 2014.

Also by Kate Tempest in Picador

Hold Your Own

Kate Tempest

Brand New Ancients

First co-produced by Battersea Arts Centre

PICADOR

First published 2013 by Picador
an imprint of Pan Macmillan, a division of Macmillan Publishers Limited
Pan Macmillan, 20 New Wharf Road, London N1 9RR
Basingstoke and Oxford
Associated companies throughout the world
www.panmacmillan.com

ISBN 978-1-4472-5768-4

9 8 7 6 5

A CIP catalogue record for this book is available from the British Library.

Printed and bound by CPI Group (UK) Ltd, Croydon, CR0 4YY

Brand New Ancients is dedicated to Camberwell, Lewisham, Brockley, New Cross, Peckham, Brixton, Blackheath, Greenwich, Charlton, Kidbrooke and Deptford, and all the gods from all those places who taught me everything I know.

Among the so-called neurotics of our day there are a good many who in other ages would not have been neurotic – that is, divided against themselves. If they had lived in a period and in a milieu in which man was still linked by myth with the world of the ancestors, and thus with nature truly experienced and not merely seen from outside, they would have been spared this division within themselves. I am speaking of those who cannot tolerate the loss of myth and who can neither find a way to a merely exterior world, to the world as seen by science, nor rest satisfied with an intellectual juggling with words, which has nothing whatsoever to do with wisdom.

JUNG: *Dreams, Reflections* (Fontana Press, 1995)

All deities reside in the human breast.

WILLIAM BLAKE

Brand New Ancients

This poem was written to be read aloud

In the old days
the myths were the stories we used to explain ourselves.
But how can we explain the way we hate ourselves,
the things we've made ourselves into,
the way we break ourselves in two,
the way we overcomplicate ourselves?

But we are still mythical.
We are still permanently trapped somewhere between the
heroic and the pitiful.
We are still godly;
that's what makes us so monstrous.
But it feels like we've forgotten we're much more than the
sum of all
the things that belong to us.

The empty skies rise
over the benches where the old men sit –
they are desolate
and friendless
and the young men spit;
inside they're delicate, but outside they're reckless and
I reckon
that these are our heroes,
these are our legends.

That face on the street you walk past without looking at,
or that face on the street that walks past you without
looking back

or the man in the supermarket trying to keep his kids out of
his trolley,
or the woman by the postbox fighting with her brolly,
every single person has a purpose in them burning.
Look again, and allow yourself to see *them*.

Millions of characters,
each with their own epic narratives
singing *it's hard to be an angel*
until you've been a demon.

The sky is so perfect it looks like a painting
but the air is so thick that we feel like we're fainting.
Still
the myths in this city have always said the same thing –
about how all we need is a place to belong;
how all we need is to know what's right from what's wrong an
how we all need is to struggle to find out for ourselves
which side we are on.

We all need to love
and be loved
and keep going.

There may be no monsters to kill,
no dragons' teeth left for the sowing,

but what there is, is the flowing
of rain down the gutters,
what there is is the muttering nutters.
What we have here
is a brand new mythic palette:
the parable of the mate you had who could have been anything
but he turned out an addict.

Or the parable of the prodigal father
returned after years in the wilderness.

Our morality is still learned through experience
gained in these cities in all of their rage and their tedium
    and yes –
our colours *are* muted and greyed
but our battles are staged all the same
and we are still mythical:
call us by our names.

We are perfect because of our imperfections.
We must stay hopeful;
We must stay patient –
because when they excavate the modern day
they'll find us: the Brand New Ancients.

See – all that we have here is all that we've always had.

We have jealousy
and tenderness and curses and gifts.
But the plight of a people who have forgotten their myths

and imagine that somehow now is all that there is
is a sorry plight,
all isolation and worry –
but the life in your veins
it is godly, heroic.
You were born for greatness;
believe it. Know it.
Take it from the tears of the poets.

There's always been heroes
and there's always been villains
and the stakes may have changed
but really there's no difference.
There's always been greed and heartbreak and ambition
and bravery and love and trespass and contrition –
we're the same beings that began, still living
in all of our fury and foulness and friction,
everyday odysseys, dreams and decisions . . .
The stories are there if you listen.

The stories are here,
the stories are you,
and your fear
and your hope
is as old
as the language of smoke,
the language of blood,
the language of
languishing love.

The Gods are all here.
Because the gods are in us.

The gods are in the betting shops
the gods are in the caff
the gods are smoking fags out the back
the gods are in the office blocks
the gods are at their desks
the gods are sick of always giving more and getting less
the gods are at the rave –
two pills deep into dancing –
the gods are in the alleyway laughing
the gods are at the doctor's
they need a little something for the stress
the gods are in the toilets having unprotected sex
the gods are in the supermarket
the gods are walking home,
the gods can't stop checking Facebook on their phones
the gods are in a traffic jam
the gods are on the train
the gods are watching adverts
the gods are not to blame –
they are working for the council
now they're on the dole
now they're getting drunk pissing their wages down a hole
the gods are in their gardens
with their decking and their plants
the gods are in the classrooms
the poor things don't stand a chance
they are trying to tell the truth

but the truth is hard to say
the gods are born, they live a while
and then they pass away.

They lose themselves in crowds, their guts are full of rot.
They hope there's something more to life but can't imagine
    what.

These gods have got no oracles to translate their requests,
these gods have got a headache and a payment plan and
    stress about
when next they'll see their kids,
they are not fighting over favourites –
they're just getting on with it.
We are the Brand New Ancients.

So choose one.
Choose any of these Gods watching telly on their own
feeling bored but not knowing what the more is to want it.
Choose one. Look again
and you will see the Gods rise
in the most human and unassuming of eyes.

Now, focus.

It's dusk on a weekday night,
kids scream and fight
in the road, cars slow at the lights
and the young men whistle at the girls, get sworn at.
Pan out slowly, draw back.
Here, this street, this road, this house,

Kevin slowly moves about,
plate down on the table, pours a stout
slow from the bottle, sits, about to eat,
we see him eye the empty chair.
Where is she? She's not there.
He checks the clock, he shrugs his shoulders,
looks down at his egg and soldiers.
The photo on the mantelpiece shows them both,
romantic beach excursion from the hazy past;
Jane is beaming, Kevin clasps her hand in his
and smiles out gently.
My wife and I, he sighs, feels empty.

So here we have them, Kevin and Jane,
Jane is bored now, ready for change,
Kevin don't see it, he's steady and plain,
the get-on-and-get-by type, don't mention your pain.
And now meet their neighbours Mary and Brian,
she's sick of his lies and he's sick of her crying
they're sick of the sight of each other, no point in trying,
they haven't been happy for years.

Well, Jane – never knew she had a body like a forest in the rain
but she felt herself change when she heard Brian say her name.
Shame ripping though her belly and her brain
leaving her in pieces with a secret to contain.
Lust, heavy in her belly, in her guts –
trust, once there, now gone, all crushed,
her marriage, robust
to the point it was gathering dust,

then her blood got hot at the thought of his touch,
but it's no big thing, it's just a crush,
right? Just
one night – it can't be love, but nights . . . weeks . . . months,
it's good, she's such a fool she hates the things she does.
She tried to call a stop to it, then woke up in a fever
sick for loving, she cannot sit still,
she's getting changed, the panic, thrill, the chill
she's lipstick in the cab, she's at the hotel bar,
she's had a couple now, she's smiling, touching, tonight
we are not wives or husbands, tonight
just us just this just crush me, finish me,
tonight man love me.

Poor Kevin – see him, dignified, steadfast, head down,
a monument to the cavalry of men who would never let down
a friend. His eyes strained from staring too long
at the empty chair while she gives herself away,
and he knows it, he feels it all day, but can't say,
See him, majestic in smallness and quiet and no fuss,
the boulder that won't budge, it crumbles inside but stays
    robust,
supportive. Kevin, your altar is covered in moss,
the inscription distorted, embossed long ago, it said once –
stay true, even if others do not.
He breaks through the rock of his silent self-loathing,
climbs into his clothing
and heads off to work. Nobody told him
to live life this way, but this is his calling,
no chaos, excitement, not romantic, enthralling

or frantic, not falling
head over heels just clawing
one hand at a time up the precipice, fighting for breath,
Kevin, a God who knows better than most how to settle
for less.

Now, bright sunlight through his windscreen, Brian's
driving home.
He just left Jane sleeping on the hotel bed.
Now it's keys in the door,
Mary's shoes on the floor,
son playing war games on the carpet. Bored of his life,
he stares at his wife,
she's got a question on her lips but knows not to ask it,
but here it is: *where've you been?* eyes full of dread and jealousy,
Brian takes off his boots and he sits down heavily.
Out, he says. She stares,
Out where?
Just out, he says.
Do we have to? Prayers
are not spoken in silence so total.
Don't push me, he says,
she knows to leave him be, she gets up slowly.
Three souls under one roof all lonely.
Brian shouts at Mary, Mary shouts at Clive,
and little Clive soaks it up with wide eyes.

Jane's baby was born in the hospital that winter at dawn,
with a full head of hair, and eyes that were warm
and inquisitive, the colour of skies in the middle of a storm.

With deliberate patience the boy grew.
Going through the kind of everyday things
just like everyday people do.
Kevin was delighted, excited, a changed man,
overjoyed and entranced,
he held the boy in his arms,
ready to be the best Dad
he could be, not knowing at all that
he wasn't. But gradually suspicion
started sneaking in –
he's got no dimple in his chin . . .
Say nothing, head down, nod and grin,
carry on, keep going. Jane stared
at the back of his shoulders in bed,
him facing the wall,
her facing the fall
from grace,
heart aching and shaking and small,
mouth full of an awful taste.
Well, working out right from wrong is never easy
when there ain't no morals,
when there ain't no justice;
when everything's weighed on the scales of profit,
it can be hard for a young man to grow up honest.
She named him Thomas.
As he grows, so does his passion for comics,
his dad is his hero, he always let him win at Sonic,
his mum teaches drawing at Lewisham College,
Tommy's a good kid, shows a lot of promise.

Mary stares out the window of the bus,
thinking of her son and how fast he's growing up.
It's hard 'cos every day that goes past,
he looks more and more like Brian, and if she's being honest
with herself, she fuckin hates Brian's guts –
she looks around and feels surrounded by young couples
still in love.
And it makes her feel small,
it makes her feel like a piece of dust
on the edge of a table top, threatened by every gust.
The flat's a state, but she can't bear to mop
the floor or put the bins out, so she just stares at the TV,
she pours a vodka into a dirty tea cup,
she's put on weight, she's miserable,
she knows that she should have a bath and clean up,
but instead she's getting pissed on her own watching the
chat shows.
She puts a pizza in the microwave and eats it off her knees.
She chain-smokes, drinking till she starts to feel quease,
and then when Clive gets home from school,
that's where he finds her, fast asleep.

It's the holidays that hurt Jane the most,
watching Kevin play with Tommy in the garden,
squirting each other with the hose –
she can see it in the boy's eyes,
hear it when the boy cries,
but she can't even begin to imagine how to apologise.
Jane – Brand New Pandora, legs crossed on the floor,
with the lid off the box,

heart full of shame and stomach in knots,
no going back, she must learn
to forgive herself and move on,
'cos what happens in love
is beyond right or wrong.

Time passes, the boys grow up. Brian's drinking
more than ever these days, he's holding fast
to the wall, about to throw up,
he's outside the pub, forehead against the railings,
a little boy walks past, skipping the cracks in the paving,
he's holding his dad's hand and Brian can hear them
    both laugh,
suddenly he feels like he's choking, he lets out a gasp –
that's him, that's Tommy . . . He straightens up, stares
at the perfect little limbs, the curls in his hair,
his mind spins, his legs sway,
he lets out a moan,
while a couple streets away
his other son is kicking up the stones on his own.

And Mary, Brand New Medea, is sat at the checkout,
beeping the items. In the deep of the night
she found the courage
to leave, but now in the cold morning light
she feels weaker and frightened, thinking –
but how will I keep Clive from hanging out on the streets?
The silence between them is already stifling.
She looks at her boy sometimes and he feels like a stranger,
she loves him but she don't know whether she likes him,

she thinks – If I cannot reach him, how can anyone
    reach him.
And if I cannot save him, how can anyone save him?
She prints the receipt and turns to the next in the line,
and here is a hero, knee deep in the desolate grind
of raising a boy to a man on her own.

And now Clive's 12, a little rotter,
mean to all the other kids. Always causing bother,
always giving someone grief. He starts off
nicking dinner money, then he nicks a bike,
then he nicks a kitchen knife
and holds up the corner shop for sweets.
Tough nut, never got enough love,
grew up in a house where his mum and dad
never said a word to each other
except when they was fighting,
that's how he learned that if you had something to say,
you said it with violence.

Tommy's 10, growing fast,
going past all the usual landmarks,
a quiet kid for the most part –
but when his hand starts sketching
it's like something's upset him,
wriggling around in his seat,
features twisting around on his face,
never really had a lot of mates,
but he would read his comic books, happy for hours,
waiting for the day when he'd discover his powers.

He'd be in class imagining the stories he'd write
when he'd get home, about all the criminals he'd fight,
and when the bell goes at last for the end of the day,
he's still in his own world, a couple dimensions away.
Jane watches her son from the school gates,
staring at the sky, looking for superman, ignored by his
    school mates,
happy though, smiling, lost in his thoughts,
and it shocks her that suddenly
she can see Brian in the way that he walks.

So now – Clive's kicking a ball
against the wall
feeling bored and angry,
and then this kid comes along,
kinda tall and gangly –
he nods at Clive, Clive stares back
says *What?* The kid nods at his ball
and says *lemme take a shot?*
Penalties? No, says Clive. *My name's Terry*,
says Terry, tackling the ball off him
and passing it back,
and they spent a couple hours like that,
till Terry's nan comes out
and shouts at him that it's dinner time,
Terry says to Clive, *I gotta go inside,*
but you can come to mine
if you're hungry? Clive looks at him briefly
like he's from another country
then he picks up his ball

and says, *alright cool.* And that's it.
Terry was Clive's first real mate.
And he cared about him, though
he'd never tell it to his face.

So one day they're round at Terry's
watching X-Men on the telly,
Terry says to Clive – *mate, if you could*
be any thing in this world
when you grow up, what would you be?
I don't wanna be nothing, says Clive, staring at the TV.
Me, says Terry, *I really wanna be a fireman.*
Clive ignores him but Terry keeps talking.
I wanna save people's lives and that,
rescue ladies from burning buildings
and carry babies down ladders
while children cheer at the bottom.
What d'you think?
Clive takes a lighter from his pocket,
fiddles with the flint, screws up some paper,
throws it in the bin.
Terry keeps talking, don't notice anything.
Sliding down that pole every time the bell goes,
be wicked wouldn't it? Clive lights the paper,
gets the bin burning,
when he sees that it's blazing
he puts it underneath the curtain,
suddenly Terry sees the fire – says,
What the fuck man? What you doing?
Clive stand up, looks him in the eye

and says to him – *Go on then, put* that *out!*
and then he runs through the door, slams it, and holds it shut
behind him. Terry stands there silent.

He looks around panicking, picks up a can of Coke –
he throws it on the flames, they just hiss and spit at him –
he can't understand why any of this happened.
The fire looks massive to him, the curtains are roaring,
he tries to throw a blanket on the blaze but he ends up falling
and getting caught in the curtains, and he's stuck,
and the fire's getting worse and it's burning,
and something's on his neck,
and it's hurting,
and he's shouting but nobody's heard him
'cos nobody's coming,
that's when he starts to cry
but then suddenly he opens his eyes
and sees Clive, he's got a bucket of water in his hand
and he throws it at the wall,
tears the burning curtains down
and stamps the flames till they're small
enough to smother, then they look at each other.
My face, says Terry, it hurts. Clive leads him out the house
with some reassuring words.
Don't worry mate, could have been much worse . . .
he puts his arm around his shoulders and sits with him on
the kerb.

In the hospital ward, Terry's taking off his bandages.
Clive's at the foot of the bed eating all his tangerines

and flicking through his magazines.
Terry's nan's in the corridor talking to the nurse.
Clive looks at Terry, asks him – *'sit still hurt?*
No, says Terry, *not really. Not much.*
He's got a scar up his neck that looks like his jaw's being
clutched
by a clawed hand. Terry says – *I don't know*
what you're doing here anyway.
I don't wanna be your mate no more.
Ah come on Terry, says Clive, *you know what I did it for,*
right? No, says Terry, *and I don't wanna know either.*
I was doing you a favour mate. How? You set my room on fire!
Well, you'll never make it as a fireman if you're scared of a blaze
like that –
you wouldn't be no good to anybody stranded in a flat,
I was trying to help you, get you prepared.
I didn't mean to hurt you. I didn't think you'd be so scared.
I weren't scared, says Terry, and for a moment he just sat there
and stared.
Maybe you was only trying to help.
And maybe I'd be a shit fireman, and I'd only hurt myself.
Underneath the hospital lights, the scar was lit up brighter
than the rest of his skin, shining, like it was still on fire.
Stop looking at it, said Terry, and his voice sounded tighter
than usual. *It's cool,* said Clive, *it looks just like a spider.*

And as they grow older Spider and Clive
spend every day side by side.
At 15, they wear the same jacket,
they walk with the same stride,

and when Clive gets in trouble
Spider's never far behind.
Then at 17, Spider sees a girl he likes,
a really smart girl who wants to put the world to rights,
she's doing A-levels, she's gonna go to uni . . .
Spider says to Clive – *mate how'm I gonna get her talking to me?*
I don't know what to say to her, every time I see her I feel stupid.
You ain't stupid Spider, says Clive, *just go do it.*
Do it now, go on, ask her how she is
and Clive shoves him in the shoulder with an affectionate fist.
Spider nods his head frantically
and walks towards her casually
hands in his pockets, and with his best gravelly voice
he says: *Alright – what's your name?*
She says *Jemma* and he feels the whole world change
he hopes she does too. He stands there for a second.
Cool. Jemma. Do you wanna, I don't know, twosie up on a fag or whatever?
She giggles. She's never seen a stranger or more desolate fella,
poor Jemma can hardly hold her shit together . . .
She grips her best friend Gloria by the arm and they burst out laughing,
and as they walk off Spider feels like such a dickhead for even asking.
Gripped by an anger and a sadness that's all new to him,
he goes and finds Clive, and for once, Clive doesn't stick the boot in him.
Instead he says *Spider, mate, people are muck –*

you either fuck them or they fuck you up.
It's you and me pal, we don't need girls or anyone,
me and you are tougher than everyone.

And so they became the bad guys,
angry, disenfranchised,
mansized
punch-happy fists, sad eyes –
but between them was decency,
between them a bond,
a shared weakness
that made them both strong.
If you see them, hoods up,
prowling the pavement at night
you'll walk quickly away,
skin prickling with terror
but they know love, though,
and they know laughter,
know each other as brother,
friend, father.
Equals. Gods in their synagogues,
an eye for an eye,
priests sharpening their steeples.
A two-man nation,
with its own rules and conventions.
Each shows respect for the laws.
One man's face is the other's reflection,
it's them against everyone when they go conquesting.
All men are weaklings, all women are whores.
And they will have their power,

two starving mouths desperate to devour,
to digest the flesh of the city
that raised them so sour,
a hunger for vengeance that never sleeps
but endures.
A hunger satisfied every night
but every morning restored.
In the old days they would have been warriors
swords singing the names of all the throats that they'd opene
but in these times they're out on the high street, smoking,
nothing to fight for but fighting itself, saying,
'It's me and you Spider. Fuck everyone else.'

Now Tommy's 19.
Walking round in a day dream
trying to work out what to do with his life:
he's a passionate painter,
he draws all through the night,
but he keeps it to himself,
he doesn't show nobody else.
He writes stories, comic book style, makes drawings,
his hero is a young man, whose life might seem boring
on the surface: by day
he works in a factory packing dog food,
but by night
he's a rebel with a devil to fight.
These days Tommy's old man don't seem to like him very mu
Tommy's parents never seem to touch.
Tommy can't bear the silence at home,
he kisses his mother on the cheek and says it's time to be gro

He gets a room in Peckham and he finds employment
working for a jobsworth prick
with a clipboard. It's telesales, it's ok,
but he lives for picking up his pen like a farmer with a pitchfork.

At 22 he finishes his first proper piece of work;
he sends it off to a publisher, his hopes and his hurts
are all there in the story, he hopes it'll work –
but the weeks stack up and the postman jerks
his head side to side, says, *nothing today mate.*
Tommy sighs deep and he goes back to bed again.
Tired eyes in a grey face, he can't work out
where life starts and his pencil ends.

She's got a far away look in her eye, like she's always had,
the kind of look that makes strangers say *it ain't so bad*
love, is it? Less flesh more spirit,
less chemistry, more physics.
Her name's Gloria,
she works behind the bar
pulling pints for the locals
down the Albert and Victoria.
She's happy in her way, she don't expect too much from life.
She believes that everybody deserves to be treated right.

She used to be a troubled type with a look in her eyes
that invited looks from the guys
that she'd meet every night in the bars
that she went to with her best mate Jemma;
they swore they were gonna be best mates forever –

they loved each other, did everything together,
they used to run riot, a couple proper little terrors.
But then Jemma stopped calling her quite so much
'cos Jemma got into going protests and stuff.
Jemma wanted the world to change,
she was 16 and smarter than most girls her age,
so while she was reading books and hanging out on picket lines,
Gloria was sniffing lines
hooking up with different guys.
Jemma wanted to go uni; she started studying hard
and the two of them just drifted apart.
Glory ran away from home when she was 17,
he was supposed to be the man of her dreams:
he had a smile like a jewel in a sewer,
knuckles like an open tool box,
eyes like Kahlúa –
he made her feel like he was the only one who ever knew her
and when he told a lie nothing ever seemed truer.
Then one day she was in a state in a heap on the floor,
wiping the blood off her jaw,
thinking I deserve more.
At the time she might have been convinced it was love
but these days, she barely even thinks of him much.
She's the kind of girl whose scars run deep
but if she smiles at you for a second it'll last you all week.

She don't compare herself to others,
she believes everybody has their own strengths;
if she was a statue she'd be less marble, more cement.

She's straightforward, no-nonsense, she just wants people
    to be honest,
she don't have no time for pretenders and she's never broke
    a promise.

But now it's Tuesday, it looks like rain;
the students are in, they're talking 'bout change.
She gives them their change;
the jukebox is playing
the same songs that it plays every day. No change.
She finishes her shift, her heart's distant, strange;
she locks up, walks home
feeling lonely, caught in the grip of the cold,
she steps into a bar, feeling old
and unloved, she orders a whisky and water
off somebody's daughter
and sits in the corner feeling awkward.

Tommy's out walking. He does it most nights.
Absorbed in the sprawl of the city, he shivers.
He feels like a Spartan in Troy.
He feels like his heart is destroyed.
Lights on in the bar across the street.
He checks his pocket for his wallet and he pushes through
    the doors.
He leans against the bar
and stares at the spirits.
25 now. Somewhere half way between
non-existent and infinite.

She's sat there thinking hard about nothing at all,
staring at the pictures on the wall.
She sees him walk in, all
self-assured self-hatred
and she thinks to herself that he's got one of them faces
that makes you want to take it
in your palms and stare at it
she looks away quickly, she don't say nothing.
He turns from the bar,
notices her hands around her glass,
struck dumb by the grace of them,
and desperate to say something.

He wakes up beside her and watches the shape of her,
breathes in the air that she breathes out.
The world is as vast and as small
as this bed, these four walls,
it's as if other than this there is nothing at all.

He likes the morning best:
the warmth of her cheek on his chest,
the light through the blinds,
the patterns it makes as it falls through the room
like it's drunk, the way he can find
new parts of her body to just sit there and hang out with,
her torso expands and retracts with her breath.
Overcome, he runs to his desk and sketches a scene,
the hero at peace with his queen.

The gods are on the beach holding hands beneath the stars
The gods are on the streets washing their cars

the gods are visiting their parents, they're talking 'bout
the past
helping their new nieces make papier-mâché masks
for the school play, the gods can't wait to have a lie in,
the gods are getting on with it, the gods are really trying.
The gods are throwing dirt on the coffin of a loved one,
blaming themselves, wondering what they done wrong;
the gods are in the kitchen making dinner for their mates,
but now they've had a row and now they've smashed a couple
plates,
the gods are up early again, working late,
standing in a queue feeling sick, got the shakes,
the gods have had enough, they got nothing left to hate,
but they like to watch the sun when it settles on the lake,
the gods are on their knees feeling lost and exhausted,
deadlines, debts, divorces,
forgotten our calling,
forgotten our wisdom,
forgotten how to speak to ourselves, how to listen.
But the gods are in the theatres, the gods are playing strings,
the gods are staring at the trees as they move in the wind,
the gods are right here, as far-fetched as it sounds:
everyone's a god, no kings, no crowns,
just us, one being, infinite and holy,
gods, messed up, lonely,
squashed, stressed out, dumbed down, raging,
wasted . . . Same as it ever was: brand new ancients.

The editor looked over his glasses.
He had a smile like dog shit hidden in grass,

complexion the colour of marshes.
He says *take a seat* and he passes a fat little hand
out for Tommy to grasp.
Tommy is nervous, all that he's ever wanted to be
is an artist, a wordsmith, a cartoonist,
and even though he kind of hates the fact
that this gross little man has the power to do this,
he's 26, he knows well enough to smile in all the right places,
this might be the chance, and he's not gonna waste it.

He takes himself out to celebrate,
allows himself the pleasure of a steak,
a nice glass of wine,
a giggle ripples up and down
the middle of his spine:
You did it! says his heart.
Shut the fuck up says his mind.

Tommy gets back to his flat and starts flicking through his
    sketches,
flicking on the telly, sipping on a beverage,
feeling like the luckiest man in the world,
counting down the hours till he can be with his girl.
He can't wait to tell her his news, he'll bring flowers,
he'll surprise her at work and together they'll walk home.
She makes him feel like a superhero in a way he's never know

Pan out, soft focus; reveal the subtext: behind
the couple striving on there is more,
the bloodspecked sword in the sand,
the bodies scattered around

like sun-bathers . . . the tattoos across their hearts read
    'when will I be famous?'

The gods are singing in the mirrors, but they're not quite
    up to par
the gods are desperate now – *please*, they say, *I wanna be*
    a star,
the gods are staring at themselves hating everything they see,
they just want to be beautiful, ageless, signed to big
labels with airbrushed bodies that shine golden,
then they can be happy; they just need to get chosen.
So choose us. The gods are on their knees before false idols
saying all I ever wanted was to make it to the final.

Polish the silverware, dust off the telly screen,
it's holy hour on Saturday evening,
the new Dionysus is in his dressing room preening,
the make-up girls hold their breath as they dream him
into a perfect bronze and then leave him
to his pre-show routine of stretching and breathing.
He winks in the mirror as he flosses his teeth,
pulls his trousers up to his nipples and strides out to the stage.
The permatanned God of our age.
We kneel down before him, we beg him for pardon,
mothers feast on the raw flesh of their children struck by
    the madness
that floods the whole country, this provocation to savagery.
Let's all get famous. I need to be more than just this.
Give me my glory. A double page spread.
Let people weep when they hear that I'm dead.

Let people sleep in the street for a glimpse of my head
as I walk the red carpet into the den of the blessed.
Why celebrate this? Why not denigrate this?
I don't know the names of my neighbours,
but I know the names of the rich and the famous.
And the names of their ex-girlfriends
and their ex-girlfriends' new boyfriends.

Now, watch him shaking his head, he is furious:
how dare this contestant have thought for a second
that this godhead, this champion of unnatural selection,
should be subjected to another version
of a bridge over fucking troubled water.
I stare at the screen and I hear the troubadours sing
the Deeds of Simon. He took the eyes from our heads
and blamed us for our blindness.

Why is this interesting? Why are we watching?

In the old stories, the gods walked among us.
Fought with each other to save us, 'cos they loved us,
or, sometimes, they turned themselves into animals,
came down upon us and raped us.
They had badness in them; they had conflicted natures.
They felt what we feel, they were imperfect and faulted
and if we excelled, we were by them exalted.
But now, we have distant pin-ups, untouchable, shining,
advertisements lying with their hands on their hearts
while we gaze up at them smiling.
But I don't want a man of the people to talk.
I want the people to speak for themselves.

And love, and be peaceful. Or if not
then incensed to anger, barbarity:
I want humanity.
I don't want this vacuous cavity
ripping the bowels out of our capacity
for quietly excellent acts.
Small heroics. Everyday epics.

It started picking up for Tommy a little at a time,
he got a little bit of hype, a little bit of recognition.
Suddenly everything was about to be different;
he'd go out drinking with these full time art guys
who made money off their work – it was more than just
    a pastime,
it was a career, it was all so clear:
he could do graphics for adverts,
make enough cash to support him and Glory
while he wrote his big story.

He got a job for a graphics PR team in the city,
specializing in advertising, young staff,
pretty receptionists, a bar in the office,
games consoles, fun team, dream job, big money,
arseholes everywhere.
Tommy was excited and challenged,
suddenly he realized that he had a talent.
He rose through the company fast making waves,
he was celebrated, he had loads of new mates
who knew how to dress and knew how to talk
and ordered the best drinks and all seemed to walk

with the confidence of Bruce Wayne without looking like
dicks
and they all knew his name and liked what he did;
and he'd come home to Glory amped up, eyes blurred,
tell her all about his day but forget to ask her about hers.
All she really wanted was for him to sit down and see her,
instead of always ranting on about his big idea.
He seemed far away, lost in a new world,
where success was round the corner and people knew
your name
before they'd met you. Gloria supported him
as best she could, but she was worried, she told him:
If they're quick to know you,
then they'll be quick to forget you.
You're talented, she said, *and I'm worried that they'll*
use you,
chew you up, spit you out, confuse you,
till you can't get your pictures out without it feeling forced,
are you sure this is what you want Tom? And he'd smile,
yeah, course.

He'd take his new mates to her pub to wait for the end of
her shift,
and she'd smile without smiling, something about them she
found so lacking,
they talked as if the future was something there for the
attacking.
She knew her Tommy so well, he had the heart of an artist,
but she couldn't make out the grain of their wood through
the layers of varnish,

they seemed unreal somehow, fake ease, she noticed that
not one of them
said please when ordering drinks, they were full of
themselves,
and it felt to her like they looked down on everybody else;
but every time they spoke Tommy grinned like a school kid
in love.
Glory sighed to herself, and got on with managing the pub.

So now it's Thursday, cold damp sky,
the night sinks down to the kerb
and it holds it tight. It's coming on twelve
and the city is thick with bodies, it heaves and it swells
and Tommy's stood in a trendy bar, feature wall
done up like a jungle scene,
complete with plastic leaves
that hang down from the ceiling
and everyone's young and clean
and fake laughing and talking far too loud.
Tommy's got his head in his hands,
they just made a deadline,
a big commission for a brand.
Everybody's backslapping, shovelling coke,
he can feel the damp drip in the back of his throat,
and he's thinking of the graphic novel that he's yet to
write,
and staring at the faces underneath the UV lights.
He was thinking – I was meant to have done so much
more with my life,
instead I got lost in this bullshit, this hype.

And here he is, 27 with a secret collection of comic book
    sketches
he can never bring himself to finish,
suddenly he sees how recently he'd let himself exhibit
the kind of traits he'd always told himself that he could
    never live with.
Coming home forgetting to be glad to kiss her,
obsessing over boardroom banter,
liquor from decanter,
quick to throw a tantrum, stressed out,
hitting his fist against the dresser,
pent up, closed off, forgetting to caress her
with the slow tenderness
that he had shown her when he'd met her.
It had become mechanical, he had to make it better.
He could see it clearly suddenly,
beneath the pressure of the strobe
against bare shoulders and ironic clothes,
glitchy pixelated smiles, sharp teeth in neat rows.
He got lost along the way, and forgot what was at stake.
Suddenly he understands, and he hopes he's not too late.

She was working the bar,
the regulars were friendly,
talking to each other,
laughing at the old jokes,
the old blokes,
too often dismissed as no hopes.
There was Sam with the squint
and the dog called Darrel,

four legs and a head
sticking out of a fluffy barrel.
Sam would have a Guinness
and get one for the dog
who lapped it from an ice cream tub at his feet,
whimpered a bit, and fell fast asleep.
There was Davey, who lived
on a diet of chips and gravy,
in the pub at noon,
he doesn't leave till 11,
he's got nothing better to do
than sit there by the window
whistling tunes.
There's Geraldine, she used to be a nurse;
she hangs out with Davey getting drunk all day,
reading yesterday's papers. These are good people by nature,
they just got worn out faces. Gloria serves them happily,
listens when they speak to her,
a lot of them don't seem to have much else,
she's a friendly face, she knows 'em all well,
they finish every order with *and one for yourself.*

The lads grab Tommy by the shoulders, say *we're off to*
Legs 11,
you've done a good job mate: call it a present.
And, just like that, jackets slung over backs,
they walk towards the door in a pack,
off to the titty bar, come on Tom, we'll buy you a dance,
they're all overblown gestures, like mime artists in France.

It's business as usual down the Albert and Vic,
Glory's helping Davey with his crossword; Twitch,
the old punk who lives on the barge, is eating a Chinese at
the bar,
while Geraldine is serenading him with *Wishing on a Star*.

But then two guys roll in round half past nine.
Gloria braces herself: they look out of their minds,
red eyes, on fire from what looks like a big binge,
speed or something much worse. She digs in her heels,
and summons the energy to offer them empathy.
She greets them. They stare back emptily;
she recognizes them but she can't place where from,
she looks away, she don't want to stare long –
she says *what can I get ya*, her smile is wider
than skies, they're hideous, pit bull necks, and dried up
saliva
each side of their mouths; she pours two ciders
and slides them across the bar towards Spider
and Clive. Now they're in the back playing pool,
the old guys are murmuring *that's Brian's boy*.
She can hear the whack of the cue,
the discs turning in the juke box,
and their cruel laughter cutting through it all.

There's a queue outside the strip bar
but Tommy's boss knows the door men
and they usher them in all big smiles
and *my friends are your friends*
and they're led to a table by a girl

with a small face and long legs.
Tommy feels weird, he don't want this, it's wrong.
Yes Tom, says one, *this is our little well done*,
he beckons to a girl, says, *over here, Michelle, come.*

She's ringing time; the regulars are leaving.
Spider and Clive are in the toilets sniffin.
She's dealt with big ugly men all her life
but these big ugly men seem different.
They're asking for one more, she tells them *closing,*
but there's a place down the road stays open till late.
Spider's got his elbows on the bar, he's leaning in close
to her face, saying *oh yeah, is that a date?*
Come on, they're saying, *one more, stop being uptight –*
we heard all about you Gloria, you're just our type.
Their faces are twisted, eyes full of spite,
looking vicious. *We'll get one for you if you like?*
You got full pints left. Gloria points to their glasses,
Finish them up, then I'm afraid that's your lot, lads.
Why you being so unfriendly? asks Clive,
you know us, we're not so bad.
She says *I don't know you,*
and I'm not being unfriendly.

The pub's empty now and no one else is there.
I like you, Clive says. *You've got nice hair.*
Spider starts giggling like a child at the fair.
Then he's stood up and he's went to the door,
pulled the bolt across and he's giggled some more.
Now Gloria's scared but she knows not to show it,

she knows bullies like these two feed off your fright.
Clive's staring at her in the murky light,
they all stand there, silent,
listening to the sound of the night.
A moment passes, she can taste its passage
on her palate, their eyes were burning,
their hands were savage –
she's seen this look before,
she knows where this is going.
They wanna do her some damage.
Come on, said Clive, *don't you wanna have some fun?*
Spider can't stop laughing, thumbs in his belt loops,
stood there at the door like a minotaur playing at a sheriff.
She's ready to fight, she knows where this is headed.

Michelle is looming over him,
staring down into his face
like she's consoling him,
but something otherworldly's
taken hold of him,
he stares at her body
and feels a sickness and a loathing
and he wants to run away
but he is stuck in slow motion.
And all he can think of is Gloria,
Gloria, the day that he met her,
the warmth of her . . .
The girl in front of him moves without thinking,
eyes glazed, hot breath on his face,
skin endless and hairless

and the room is so airless
and he feels so small and distressed
and so distant and nothing is real or alive,
it feels like he's looking up from beneath water,
she's rubbing her thighs and staring with eyes
that don't seem to be open, face painted and monstrous,
sexy by numbers. While in his guts Gloria calls him, like
    hunger.

He can hear himself saying, thanks, great, good to see you.
Autopilot schmoozing, being charming, feeling see-through.
And now at last, he's walking out fast, the air is cold against
    his face,
his heart sings her name, he's running like he's being chased
to the station, finds a tube, and the world is small and he is
    drowning
and all he wants to do is find her and have her wrap her
    limbs around him.
The tube becomes a chariot of fire,
and his heart is renewed with an honest desire,
his shoes become wings and he flies towards her side,
to throw himself before her and promise he will try
with new vigour to be better,
to be bigger, he is baptized in the sweat of his fury,
he runs and his breath beats the drums
of the night into rhythms
that sing *please forgive him . . .*
He sees the city through the prism
of her image, all Glory all Golden,
all her and he's hoping

and brand new and part of the chaos
he ran through, thinking, *yes,*
I have strayed and my heart was betrayed
by my pride and my ego, but through my love I am saved.

And he turns onto the street at last, the pub is steady in
the distance;
and he can feel himself twice the size he was before – legs
move like pistons,
eyes full of a new conviction,
off to find the girl he loves
and say to her with honest words
I know I've not been good enough.

She felt the atmosphere turning . . .
She's known trouble all her life,
she can spot it from a mile off
in the way a smile drops from off a face.
Clive's breath is so bad she can taste it,
he stares at her, she stares back;
the stares were weighted, as they waited
for a sign that the time had come, and then it came,
Clive pushed himself upon her,
eyes full of agony and shame:
she felt his hatred, she felt his hand around her throat,
and it was ancient.
Spider's breath was coming hard,
he was watching from the door
as Clive pushed her against the bar
and threw the glasses to the floor.

He was swearing at her and at himself.
She looked him in the face,
intent on discovering some tiny trace
of grace, some snatch of goodness . . .
but there was nothing.
Only cheeks puffing,
she could feel him rubbing on her,
a scream gathered in her stomach
and she heard it coming from her,
for every time she'd found herself numb
before the pounding fists of some
disgusting monster, she came to life now,
she found her wits, for every lie she'd been told,
for every time she'd been beaten down, used and made weak –
she called upon that weakness now
for Tommy's silent stares
looking past her, looking through her,
for every one who's ever fucked her over.
Clive was close to her,
one hand on her shoulder,
the other opening his flies,
she felt the fury rise,
stared straight into his eyes;
he couldn't meet her gaze
but she wouldn't look away.
She reached behind her head
and pulled a bottle from its place,
swung the bottle in his face
and he just grinned while it hit him
though he bled like something bit him . . .

She swung again, the bottle smashed,
she stuck it in him. He was almost laughing,
blood bubbled at his temple, he kept grasping,
eyes rolling, breath rasping.
She grabbed another bottle, swung them both;
he was throttling her throat.
They fell to the floor, he was above her, so close she felt
smothered
but she recovered her senses, kicked out with her knees,
stuck the bottle in him and twisted till she felt him bleed.

Tommy got to the pub, found the door locked,
went round the back and he knocked;
it was open, he went in whistling . . .
That's when he saw Spider by the door,
Gloria on all fours, Clive on the floor –
her eyes were all force as she let out a roar,
he saw a rage he'd never seen before.
Frozen to the spot, summoning the heroes he used to
draw . . .
But his supermen abandoned him,
the shock of it anchored him,
he couldn't move a muscle –
he felt like he was dreaming, found himself weeping
to the sounds of her shrieking
but unable to move he was stood there,
invisible and useless
as Glory burned brighter than any one of Zeus's daughters,
the fight in her eyes was inspiring.
He saw her, the quiet resolution, the timing,

her steadfast compassion that kept her beside him
and he saw her as if for the first time: fire in her eyes shining.

Clive was off her, she stopped screaming.
Spider stood still, breathing hard;
she felt like she was dreaming,
saw her face reflected in the broken shards.
She could feel him thinking,
sensed he was about to charge –
Clive was muttering and still,
Spider's eyes were dark and large.
Then he ran towards her.
Her anger was total and abrupt,
she was sick of being shitted on
and she didn't give a fuck –
she struck Spider round the head
then stuck the bottle in his guts,
he dragged her down with him,
kicked her face
but she sprang up to stand above him
and spit into his eyes from a bloodied mouth,
she could feel the desperation of a lifetime coming out.
It was like she'd reconnected with a strength she had forgotten
she possessed.
Her heart beat like wings in her chest.

She was silent now, she stood still, staring at them with the
bottle by her,
They were breathing, Spider whimpered like a puppy in a fire.

Tommy couldn't speak, but he walked gently from the
wall,
she turned to see him there, feeling like she was about
to fall.
And she had nothing much to say to him
but they put their arms around each other,
and he held her trying to tell her
with his arms everything that he'd discovered
on that journey on the tube and in that moment when he'd
watched,
her defending herself like a heroine, a god.
And with his eyes he apologized for every night
he hadn't kissed her right.
And he knew that he was understood 'cos he felt her hold
him tight.

The Gods are waking up and reaching for their partners,
the gods are raising kids doing PhDs and Masters.
The gods are having physio, learning how to walk after
a fall,
the gods are feeling miserable and they don't know who
to call,
the gods are lying on the floor feeling far away and
worthless,
the gods have forgotten that they're gods, that they're
perfect.
The gods are holding one another in the darkness of
the pub,
a god becomes a god when it has got the guts to love.
A god remains a god for ever, no matter what it does,

but still, a god should try and be the kind of god a god
can trust.
There are no clear-cut definitions of what's just,
every god has got it in them to crush, to be crushed,
to fall, to rise up, to give far too much, to take beyond
taking, to hate, but the main thing is 'great' is a state of mind.
We are ancient, brand new, basic and far beyond making
ourselves into nothing; we need to recognize we're something,
and that we can be the gods we were born to be through
loving.

Yes, the gods are on the park bench, the gods are on the bus,
the gods are all here, the gods are in us.
The Gods are timeless, fearless, fighting to be bold,
conviction is a heavy hand to hold,
grip it, winged sandals tearing up the pavement –
you, me, everyone: Brand New Ancients.

Shadows and rain and a man going nowhere.
Brian's watching the shapes in the dark, his glass full of
whisky;
his mind on the years that he ran through,
he didn't know at the time how the days that he drank to
would flood him and sink him when he came to be sixty.
But now here he is, alone in his flat in the dark with a whisky.
All his young loves have grown up to be loved by much better
men,
at the time he forgot 'em so easy; but now there was no
forgetting them.

The dark clung to the trees in the garden like wet clothes,
he remembered, Mary, fully dressed in the sea,
with her legs round his waist
and her breasts in his face
and now here he was
all alone with his specs
and his excess flesh
his bad breath
in a mess,
in a state.

They'd had a son called Clive but Clive hated his guts
for being drunk all the time when he was raising him up;
he'd thrown punches at Clive, left him grazed, left him cut,
till one night, he had stayed late at the pub
and he'd come home to find no one was there –
Clive and his mum had packed up and left. He sat down in
his chair
and he took a deep breath. He was a man going nowhere,
what could he expect?

There was another kid too, he had had an affair;
Jane was lovely, bright red hair –
it's not like he didn't want to care
but when Jane came to him, tearful, scared,
and said let's me and you leave town and start
a family, he just couldn't want it.

That was years ago now. Still, his misery deepened;
every night that went by he would get less sleep and

after a time he said *I can't bear this,*
every day I'm getting closer to the care home, the stair lift,
his memories teased him, he was lonely, miserable,
days into weeks, all alone feeling pitiful.

He was an old man now,
no family to bring warmth
to his dirty little flat, it made him sad to think
of all the women who had loved him who he never had
    the guts
to love back.

He'd worked thirty years at the airport,
one of her majesty's henchmen,
and now he was drawing a pension.
So one day he packed up a bag and he boarded a plane
and he flew far away from his disgrace and pain.

Now, SuChin was lovely, sexy, young and sweet;
she'd smile at him when they would eat
their lunch together on the beach
and he could feel himself becoming something.
Shaking off a life of being worse than nothing,
he knew people thought of men like him as disgusting –
but he didn't care. He found happiness there
and even an old man deserves some loving.

He ain't blind and he ain't dumb.
He knows it's his money that buys her kisses.
He also knows that poverty is vicious,

and that to her entire family, he makes all the difference.
Besides, back home he's living hand to mouth,
but out here, his pension is riches.

He used to spend his time in bars and pubs where he would pour his heart out
to barmaids, compensating for his lack of friends by drinking till he passed out.
But here, in paradise, this fair Olympus where he'd come to live,
he had a bunch of mates just like himself: Ian, Graham, Sid.
All of them were old Western men with young Thai girls by their side.
They would all go for drinks together, sometimes motorcycle rides.
And it made him feel like a teenage heart throb, a catch, a superman,
with his big white belly hanging over his trunks and a bottle of brew in hand.

And now he sat, out on his porch.
The sea was flat, the air was warm;
he thought back on his life and its miserable course
and he felt the unfamiliar pangs of shame and of remorse.
But no dark old cloud could reach him here,
he felt no anger, felt no fear,
he was just an old man, with
a nice young girl to hold hands with.
A single tear slid out his eyes, his nose ran.
He thought of Clive, poor Clive. And poor Tom.

He never met his youngest son
and he felt terrible for the things he'd done,
how he'd never been there to teach them right from wrong
and he wondered what kind of things went on for them:
young men now, tall and strong.
And he hoped they weren't as foul as him,
and his heart was broke and his hair was thin,
he felt the pain of all his sins
and he thought of Mary, young and slim,
dressed up nice on a date with him
and he thought of how he'd made Jane sing
in bed together and he ached –
his flimsy morals seemed to shake
and whimper, poor old Mary, poor sweet Jane, poor
    young Clive,
so big and strange, and poor quiet Kevin, and poor
    little Tommy.
Brian felt a sickness in his head and a lightness in his body,
he drank deeply, and *poor old me . . .*
when I was young, all the things I'd hoped I'd be
I never was, but here I stand,
I've done what I've done, I've lived. I'm a man.
He raised a glass to the dark skies,
sipped his whisky, smiling wide
then he thought of SuChin with her lovely eyes,
chuckled to himself and he quietly died.

Acknowledgements

I would like to thank India Banks for all her advice, criticism and encouragement. Without you Indie I would never have started or finished this poem. Thank you for everything you do all the time.

Huge thanks also to Nell Catchpole, Kwake Bass, Raven Bush, Natasha Zielazinski and Jo Gibson for working so hard on creating such a perfect score.

And thanks to Sophie Bradey and all at the Battersea Arts Centre for their help and time and belief in the story.